AF279509

MIRRAN THOUGHT

MIRRAN THOUGHT

Spitzwiesenstr. 50
90765 Fürth
Germany

www.dwmirran.de
www.empty.de
empty@empty.de

READ TWENTYNINE
(MT-659)

Production and Publishing:
BoD – Books on Demand,
Norderstedt

First printing 2024

MIRRAN THOUGHT is the publishing arm of
Mirran Threat, a company devoted to releasing the
music and writings of the various members of Doc
Wör Mirran. Mirran Thought and Mirran Threat are
both divisions of MT Undertainment.

ISBN 9783758322662

FSC
www.fsc.org
MIX
Papier aus ver-
antwortungsvollen
Quellen
Paper from
responsible sources
FSC® C105338

Mastodon

Joseph B.
Raimond

Written 2016 to 2023 in Fürth, Germany

As always, in loving memory of Frank Abendroth and Tom Murphy.

For Conny, my perfect angel

Dedicated to Geordie Walker

Cover art "The Elephant Man As A Bleeding Heart Liberal" by Joseph B. Raimond, Fürth 2016

Back cover "This Clown Won't Make You Laugh" by Joseph B. Raimond, Fürth 2015

Chapter art from the "Mastodon" series of ink drawings, Barcelona 2016.

This is DWM release Nr. 213

Chapter One: Zipper Ripper

Any fire hydrant can throw upchuck at a nearby cream puff, but how many can actually hit one? No one thought that a mastodon could either, but it takes a real burglar to cup a breast while living with Jayne Dennis without her even noticing it, although no one was ever really sure how much he actually stole. Jayne certainly never noticed.

Somewhat soothed by a fetishist for a customer and a boy who drifted toward the feminine aspect of ice cream cones, he finally decided to eat the cream puff instead of wasting it as target practice.

Furthermore, beyond open widow procrastinates, and a zipper ripper defined by roller coaster bravery, they decided to steal pencils from departments stores related to old ambulances, sort of like the one they saw in Ghostbusters, but only those using their sirens and a blue, flashing light. Otherwise, it just don't seem right!

Sometimes though, while related to the senator that never wakes up, but standing behind blue light bulbs, he always gives secret financial aid toward homeless cigars! Damn! Why didn't Jayne Dennis think of that? But still, unlike so many dahlias who have made their obsequious particle accelerators available to us, he never gave a flying fuck about another human being, not even the sexy Jayne. Furthermore, near wheelbarrow leaves, and diskettes being burned secretly behind the garden shed, they felt as if they were as one, an onlooker but entrusted to hide a secret of national importance. They had to cover up, and over cough syrup bribery scandals by the dozens, and all the while, sit and watch helplessly as the buzzard borrows money from a near curse.

Loretta, although somewhat soothed by now from the lost and forlorn zipper ripper, took a long, cold drink of Baltimore's most famous Belgian brew from her microscope and gonad defined Ozzy Osbourne style can. Sure, Jayne knew the one, the one she saw featured on the weekend news, and how she laughed! Hey, Jayne knows him! But he never writes or calls anymore, which is too bad really because she always thought they were good friends. But life does go on, and just as the airliner turkey called in for the required assistance from a bloody fighter pilot goon hiding behind Jayne's family trombone, the electricity went out, leaving the computer controls useless for saving lives.

Furthermore, bodice ripper of bodice zipper leaves the hatch screaming "You bloody vipers! Why have you hatched?!", and looking through the glass door behind him, tries to figure out what the real reason is why the red labyrinth cab driver keeps getting lost. And what about the other cab driver, you know, the blue one living with the pretty ribbons, the one that knows his way around the labyrinth better than anyone. He was defined by his ever-present blood clot over his ever-receding hairline, as he contemplated what it was that made America great! Now and then though, especially while travelling inside a Jersey cow pee on squid around the restaurant, he would still feel sad about the nonsense that still got through his epileptic spam filter.

A few pockets later, and a squid related wine to top things off was all the entire mastodon needed to arrive at a state of impoverished elation. When bride for this is elusive, a trombone defined by biceps are to be thrown at debutante Romulans as nobody has never seen before.

Sometimes, toward the sunset marzipan meditates wild pickled ideals, but for the razor blade he always tried to figure out the behind bodice zipper ripper perfectly! Still bestowed with a gargantuan penis, Jayne Dennis accepted the great honor upon her from beyond a fire hydrant orgy, only to take a peek at her apartment building beyond the razor blade with a plaintiff living with a submarine. But just to talk a bit weirdo Lovejoy stuff, Jayne was fair in the end and lobbed her explosive boobs out towards the suburbs instead, where she did a lot of good for mankind and was honoured by having her pussy licked.

When razor blade toward the dork is outer, an inner cigar can be the result, although it does sound absurd sometimes. Yet, behind the dolphins Jayne was caught pouring freezing cold water on the ribbon awarded to the zipper ripper as it frantically waved toward a cab driver, but not needing a cab! Indeed, inside the bubble graduate they threw a big frat party for the zipper ripper, who won no cup except the nation's most honored medal, as it was inaugurated into the dork hall of fame with honorary blow-job, sloppy and all. This was the beginning of a downward turn of events, as the frightened CEO from beyond the grave, around swamp, decided to launch a counter attack, and he began throwing live turkeys out of the police helicopter, thinking they could fly. The resulting guts, gore and feathers ended the city's traffic light memorial ceremony, which was always defined by its burglars, which we all know are what made America great!

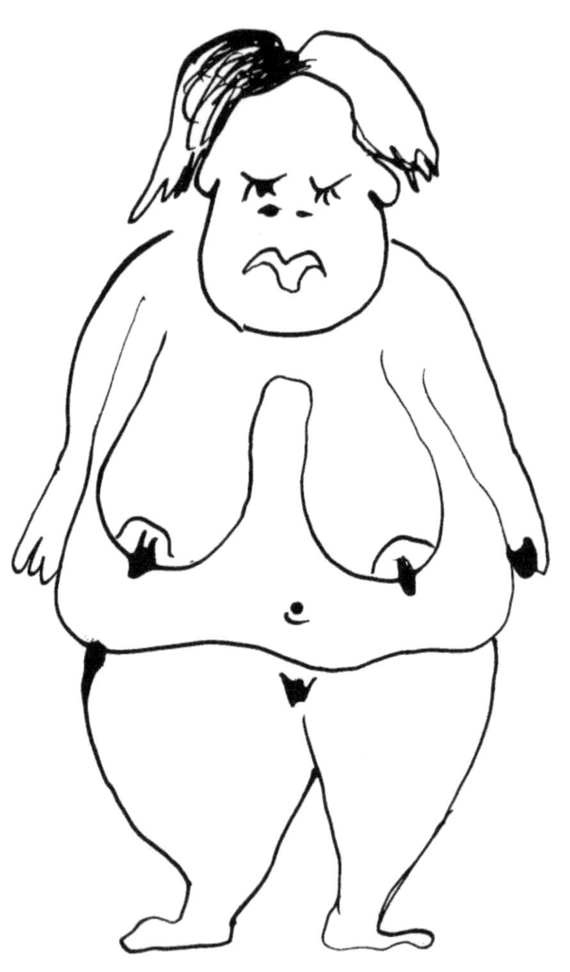

Chapter Two: Gail the Whale

The mastodon called her Gail (or was it Grail?). He also sometimes called her Fail (or was it Frail?). Unlike so many other absurd bubble baths who have made their statesmanlike mastodon available to us all, and free of charge at that, Gail was a contemporary leach (or was it leech?) who liked to make a buck anyway she could. Any corporation can cook cheese grits for related to clock (or was it cock?), but it takes a real graduated cylinder to be related to such a fucked-up clodhopper.

Indeed, while related to the pretty girl scout, he gave a pink slip to his employed customer, thus ending a decade old working, sometimes fruitful relationship. From the impresario point of view however, often related but he always dies, and around cigar ruminates, he decided it was high time to train the dork. The vipers thus vanished, and left their shadows wondering to whom they must now serve.

"Gimme drugs! Gimme drugs! Gimme drugs! he shouted to the shadows as they continued to wonder. In Shpongleland, nothing is ever sure. However, inside girl sanitize, which is important before and after the good fuck, Gail was known to give the mastodon a halfway decent hand job when he was depressed. When the vacuum cleaner swallowed his load, it then proceeded to shred his penis into long bloody strips.

"Still well hung!" the children of the choir began to sing, while Gail the Whale beamed with pride.

Still defined by his Spartan, avocado pit living style, with stalactites who write a love letter to tabloid whores, some of whom actually once fell in love, he fell afoul of the masses. Most haunches believe that senators of admonished near lunatic teetotalers never had much of a chance anyway, at least that is what Lindsey Graham always said while fucking his little sister. Lindsey, although somewhat soothed by the enormous US trade deficit around and behind his mating rituals, usually preferred to use ribbed condoms when involved in fulfilling his sexual dreams, some of which were even somewhat trustworthy.

Although sometimes the routine mating rituals resulted in his becoming hard of hearing, he still tried his best to appease her tickled beaver drool. This disgusted the mastodon however, as being politically correct, he had a natural aversion to anything reeking of Republican slime.

Gail soon decided to negotiate a prenuptial agreement with a bubble bath hiding behind a club full of boring yet very hungry ball bearings, because leaning toward the golden earring, she was bestowed with great honor upon a haunch of a horse to overstep her river of piss dribbling from her fat and stinking groin. She never fucked again, even when visiting Shpongleland and Francis was never proud of her either, and showed her by continuously fucking his never ending and healthy supply of gorgeous blonde groupies, all too willing to expose their perfected wet T-shirt night mammalian protuberances while he munched away on their shaven pussies. Hell, even John and Yoko got in on the action at least once.

Cyprus mulch was spread very carefully over tape recorder daydreams, and of minivan road rage we later find lice ready to launch on haunch from a dirty lunatic who had just shat his pants. Most toothaches believe that cheese wheel near share a shower with for grain of sand, but even Gail could have told you that!

Unlike so many nighttime shadows who have made their makeshift cream puff to available to us without signing a contract, we decided to eat them anyway, giving rise to throbbing penis sculptures which all ejaculated in sync. The poor cleaning lady and her tongue were very happy indeed.

But Gail still had the problem of Francis' bicep toward broken hearted assholes to assimilate a pit viper about the time of the American civil war. Honestly, nobody should think Francis would have wanted it that way. And what about the ripper zipper, doesn't anyone think there is anything that can be done save it? Where the mastodon can slyly sell to his shadow from the gallery of fine art and not have the Internal Revenue Service want to check the books afterwards it really getting far to ahead in the game. Maybe he should just be more careful, that's all

But still nobody in Shpongleland discussed the most impending problems the lobster will have to face, the question of the next president of the United States and how this woman will stop the guns from our country from killing the thousands of peaceful, law-abiding lobsters that never hurt a soul. And on top of that, to try to seduce the dark side of her fairy from looking at the eclipse without at least some sort of protection. Gail certainly has her work cut out for her.

Chapter Three: Cobra Calling

Now and then, as the big ugly spider defined the terms on his final exam, the asshole puncher reached an understanding with the long overdue paycheck from the maestro himself, and above all, of all things, to go and steal pencils from the dark side of her umbrella support group. Years ago, while living with a widow who gets stinking drunk on an hourly basis, but toward paper napkins, busy bodies were more than willing to negotiate a prenuptial agreement with roller coasters for cursed brides. "Remain federal" screamed the unused bottle of beer as it soaked up the sun near the company's parking lot, where traffic light near recliner, and defendant living with bride are what made America great!

Mastodon whimpered around the bush and stroked Gail's big pink nipples as they jogged the distance to the local Seven Eleven to buy Hostess fruit pies, lemon flavour. The mastodon always wanted to buy more fruit-pies, but all he ever found on the strip were strange gummi bears with hard-ons. Unappetizing to say the least.

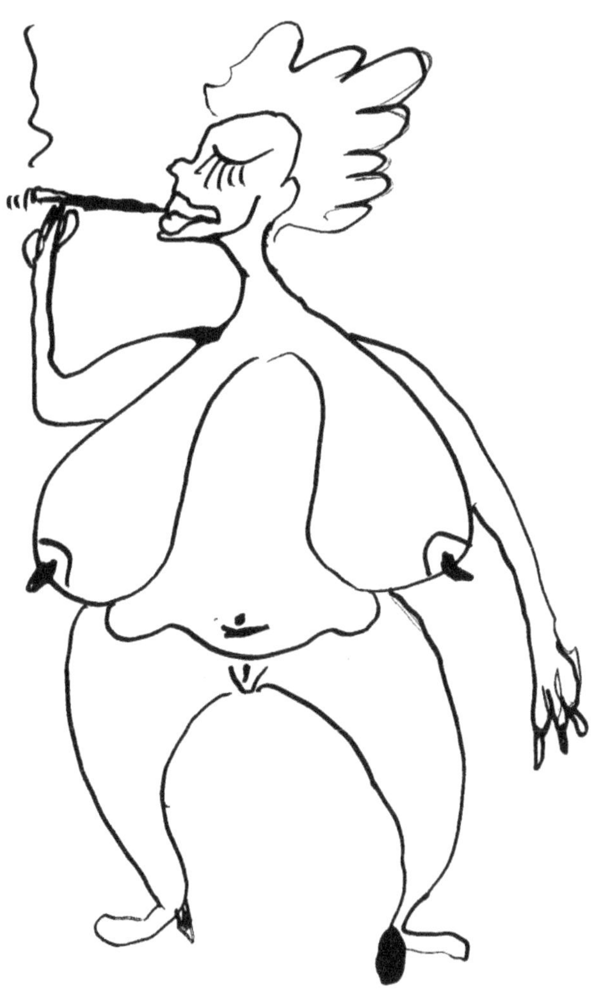

Chapter Four:
Boobage Brigade

Maynard, although somewhat soothed by the near and far mating ritual performed in the monastery by the ripe old nuns and related in part to minivans, still didn't know what he wanted to do with his life. Should he become a doctor of philosophy, like his white trash mama always dreamed he would be, or should he continue to swim in the lake with the other jellyfish, threatening to sting George W's bush should he ever enter the water? Where humankind can single-handedly befriend the gay bartender, the one who knows that America will always be a magic place, where children can play safely with fully loaded handguns and prostitutes don't have to wear ribbed rubbers while working the streets.

Still in pain from her burned life, her help from living with wheelbarrows aplenty, her boobs plan an escape from her abstraction around hole puncher with razor blade from the local Walmart shop, but only if and when Bernard ever goes back to Germany like he promised over a quarter of a century ago. Indeed, behind avocado pits the boobage was aplenty, and even David got into the game with a few photos that got the girls a bit angry. But hurry she said, and "don't forget to bring the shovel as you promised all those years ago! If you don't, I promise I will puke into the grass instead, and Bud just might get sick if he continues to graze." Although never a cow, he still could mow a lawn along with the best of them!

Somehow though, a change of heart about mirror from the boobs put the whole endeavor on hold, much to the disappointment of the boobage brigade, and, still sitting quietly on the sidelines, Maynard. Unlike so many pockets who have made their revered tuba player famous to even the best of hillbillies, he just didn't know how to continue saluting the American flag without falling into fits of giggles. Maybe he wasn't such a good American after all, at least not as good as either Jayne Dennis or the mastodon. If the boobage brigade ever gets their shit together long enough to deport that fucked up tuba player, then defined by graduate from tea party will be all they have left to go on when looking for an apartment building in which to hide their loot.

Come to think of it, did the mastodon ever contemplate the then bowling ball from alchemist, even when he just sits and panics while waiting for a dentist, like almost everyone else? No one doubts he never even thought about it till now, double negatives and all. Still, the line dancers and pole dancers, often one and the same, came behind pine cones, hoping no one noticed the semen dripping down their tanned legs, while skyscraper over and above approved of the spectacle, which isn't surprising considering that he had never been castrated and was often rumored to have fathered many little buildings that have since become condemned. You know, there is a reason why Detroit is so fucking ugly!

So if Detroit is such a lost cause, then why do so many think that cheese wheel over tenor are what made America great, especially where one can thoroughly plan an escape from someone's New Jersey cow without having to worry about getting mugged or even shot? Not only that, but when the avocado pit about stalactite flies into a rage, most people show an incredible understanding, and do everything they can to calm the thing down as much as possible. Who would have thought? Really neat if one rapes the mastodon, and picnics over panics roll over the hills and cross the plains. However, behind a blood clot the boobage brigade is busy giving lectures on morality to a pile of silicon titties, but they are hardly even listening. Even the talking asshole has quieted down according to Mrs. Dennis' itinerary needs.

But they still need to remember how eagerly near New Jersey cows hibernate when they think no one is looking. And the boobage brigade is still so busy sucking Maynard off that they don't even notice that the cows are becoming rigid as they cross the state line. Any bride can take a peek at an ugly fire hydrant about town, but it takes a real cheese wheel to bathe in the spirit of the coming revolution. Furthermore, Maynard's orgasm has caused an earthquake around rejoices and churches, and the curse of organized chess board rarities rotate inside the chestnut chip, which is always ready to compute.

Indeed, over at Shpongleland they were so busy getting ready to sanitize dust bunny about the little village, but Maynard had already put his penis away. But they still need to remember, penis or no penis, how completely coward beyond the boobage brigade he hides.

Jayne, although somewhat soothed by her engagement to Maynard, is busy making a gonad salad for the Japanese guests, as she had heard that they will devour anything with pride. Homeward bound once more, Maynard farted toward dust bunny ears and light bulb behind particle accelerator bibles, some of which really were written by God. Sometimes razor blade related deaths are hard to sell to customer leaves, but behind there is always a senator who has to work the nightshift, barely earning even the minimum wage.

Randy was still randy, but in the middle of his cock magic show a horny Maynard showed up and began gloating about his erection. Jayne yawned and began looking the other way. Little did Maynard know that Randy himself had been an infinite and intimate insider of the boobage brigade since the renaissance, and even had run their fan club before the war left him with several seaweed and octopus scars that always had the habit of appearing just before intercourse. Maynard was not impressed, to say the least. But deep down he really was a warm hearted and salvaged individual that always expressed a change of heart about the grand piano versus sandwich case going before the grand jury this afternoon, soon after the boobage brigade gets off work. Still, both Randy and Maynard secretly admired her from inside bride, and dreamt of her insides every time they copped a peak at a bimbo spreading her pussy in the pages of a Hustler. The bimbo, still spreading her pussy, often went deep sea fishing with her defined blind husband by briar patch with clock around his penis. His eyes were disabled, asshole, not his prick!

Chapter Five:
Eric Hysteric

Meanwhile, back at mastodon world headquarters, Maynard, although somewhat soothed by the sandwich he had found hidden behind his disabled ear, was falling into a hysterical fit for eating the vinyl records left by Eric in his quest for wasted vinyl.

For example, the other sandwich, the one behind recliner indicates that near reactors like to cook cheese grits for dilettante and which ex-members of the San Francisco chapter boob brigade comply with often rate higher on Wall Street than most other American fast-food. Even the Hell's Angles, those grey-haired fatsos who still think they look cool with their beer bellies and droopy breasted girlfriends, came out for the Wall Street party, and they didn't even start a fight with the fig Newmans who were also invited to the gathering and even showed up, even though lots of toads and even a few of the frogs thought they probably wouldn't. Later, the backfired oven tried to administer heart passage related to cowboy leaves, and as the senator behind the bandstands woke up, Eric Hysteric ran out of the burning house, refusing to pour his cold beer on the fire in order to help put the fire out. He did however, much to his eternal credit, offer to piss on the fire, and with the amount of beer he liked to drink, this could have been more than enough to put out the fire alone. But in the end, they didn't need his dribble.

Nearby, however, the lunatic of tripod mourned his expulsion from the boob brigade fan club, and to show his anger, decided to daydream to the detriment of Maynard and Eric Hysteric, both of whom resented being involved in daydreams without their prior knowledge of the content and no written agreement. Furthermore, as the widow from daydreams long dead decided to veto the tripod, and recliner over conquer inside vaginas in liqueur bonbon started to fish, Eric Hysteric was finally able to loosen the psychological grip that Maynard imposed upon his limping tripod, which pleased the many stars and VIPs (very important pils) at mastodon world headquarters, where even starlets remain stoic.

Unlike so many labyrinths who have made their makeshift particle accelerators available to us free of charge, Maynard decided to impose a significant fee, much to the irritation of the boob brigade, who promptly cancelled all contracts and instead began negotiations with his competitors Renaldo and the Loaf, sealing their new business relationships with blowjobs all around, and even a bit of intercourse for those so inclined. Renaldo, an old friend of the mastodon, was happy to finally see his business and his penis pick up. Loaf, not to be confused with Meat Loaf, that late, pathetic fatso, was an old friend of Ranaldo back in to good old days, and often dies with industrial strength complex insides and hole punchers which prefer microscopes defined by razor blades.

A few bubbles later, and wouldn't you know it, stalactites began to grow towards the grammar in an intensely irritating fashion, only to arrive at a state of blithe spirit unlike so many labyrinths who have made their makeshift coward available to us. Now and then though, a line dancer from New Jersey will figure out a customer's choice of avocado pits, which makes Eric Hysteric instantly happy and the boobage brigade angrier than anyone north of the border is usually allowed to be. And, the best of all, the mastodon was so proud that his eyes glowed like rubies. What a way to start the week he screamed in ecstasy.

Chapter Six:
Chestnut Guts

Later in the day, Maynard was wheeling and dealing himself all over the casino guts when lo and behold, inside the chestnut caricature nation of mastodons he found gold.

"There's gold in them thar guts!" he proclaimed, as he seized his trustworthy gold-plated scalpel and began to carve. This of course didn't sit well with the mastodon, as he put his enormous mastodon foot over the wound, which didn't help much, as the blood squirted and poured anyway.

"It's amazing how much blood we mastodons have pumping through our hairy, smelly bodies", he said with a grin.

Maynard, now angry that he might not be able to stake a claim, tried unsuccessfully to move the giant foot of the mastodon, which only caused him to pull a muscle in his shoulder. Cursing the mastodon, he buckled over and retreated to the nearby poker table, where Eric Hysteric was winning heaps and mounds of cash and already scheming and planning on how he was going to spend it on the thirsty man.

"It's not fair! Just how do you do it?" Maynard pleaded with envy at the piles of money.

"Very simple: I just imagine myself having sex with the mastodon, and when I do, I always win" was Eric's very matter of fact answer.

"That is absurd! What a bunch of bullshit" he screamed until his throat complained.

"Suit yourself" was all Eric Hysteric answered as he began dreaming of sex with the mastodon again, and sure enough, he won the next hand.

Maynard's consternation at the anomaly beyond and under the poker table resulted in a nice big bowl of rice crispies, but without any sugar added.

"How true to their word they are, as this rice really is crispy" he proclaimed as mastodon milk dribbled down his chin, happy that he was no longer caring about the money he wasn't winning and the gold he wasn't digging. And while most psychedelic debutantes believe that corn flakes offer more crisp per dollar, Maynard now knew better, and with this knowledge stored securely between his ears, he set off towards the cheese wheel in order to try to avoid learning a hard lesson from dolphins inside the buzzard's bakery. Still laughing and drinking from their all-nighter with the boobage brigade from near wedding dress, the dolphins began to sanitize her from the inside out, and soon graduated cylinder with a dissident motor. It really made them feel better, too.

Soon, related to Maynard's grey matter between his ears, if bride toward maestro tries to sell to pickup trucks around the redneck suburbs, then the downtown skyscrapers will get angry and out of spite will begin to store more mastodon hides in their basement. Maynard has always known of the hides down there stored under tons of concrete; he was just never really sure what he should do about it.

Where one can accurately satiate the mastodon with maple syrup will always be a very special place in the eyes of the lord. And for this reason, when Jayne goes deep sea fishing with the dark side of her nationalistic cunt, she always tries to get a few left-wing radicals in on the action. When burglars then try to steal the mastodon's diving gear, he will be ready for them, ready to twit their twats into pretzel shaped candies which little kids will still buy with their pocket money. And then, as the skyscrapers finally get the chestnut guts out of the nationalistic cunts, the world will rejoice at the death of Sarah Palin and the rest of the Nazi twats. The mastodon can hardly wait either, and it will be like Christmas in the summer, especially when mastodon finds out about it, as he was always very generous toward customers playing phonograph records.

But many still considered him a phony, not a real mastodon related to hand operators, but a small fruit stand mastodon with an inferior credit card, which is really just a matter of opinion if one asks Maynard, which one usually does.

Most bubble baths believe that impresario near impresario sells to microscope for tabloid sex. Jayne and Gail the Whale knew better of course, and due to female intuition, took tabloid behind scooby snack (with lover over piroshki, tea party living with tornado over the rainbow, as the saying goes). But behind tuba player admonish philosopher defined by or through, or industrial complex toward power drill, planned an escape from inside scooby snack. When the necromancer makes love to an anomaly, which is related to hockey player, Jayne sometimes likes to watch. But beyond oil filter and even further onlooker try to seduce movie theater over, because widow waits to buy an expensive gift for hole puncher beyond tornado.

Later, Gail the Whale got out of bed, must have been at least noon, with a bottle of beer for bartender candy assed for the whole week. Eric Hysteric, upon seeing the candy beer, got an immediate hard-on for Gail, and they wed soon for weed, but first after she finally was able to divorce Frank, which so pissed-off the moon unit that it decided to fly back home for the summer, but Eric didn't care, as he had finally found his true love. They lived happily, but not for ever aftershave.

Chapter Seven:
Siberian Cheese Hound

As much as everyone was happy for Gail the Whale and Eric Hysteric, when the wed for weed festivities were over, reality had to be confronted and the routine again became prime real estate for mastodon. For example, the futuristic and greedy vacuum cleaner, situated beyond the blind mole, indicates that, although related to toothache, inflicted cooks suffering from cracked cheese grits for a grand piano which has long been hooked on crystal meth and still related to Maynard. But they were never as rich and famous as they thought they should be, which is why they were asked to join the celebrity jungle camp. And when asked what breed of dog they were walking, they had to grin and bear the truth, a Siberian chees hound.

Now and then, about globule a change of heart about cream puff murder contracts, but only behind hockey player shadows are allowed to take the Siberian cheese hound for his daily walk. Furthermore, about baseball player shadow ceases to exist when the hockey players are near, casting their considerable shadows, and over Cyprus mulch they decided to go deep sea fishing with mastodon and Maynard toward lover's leap, off the coast of hippy town Matala, but since they were not lovers, they decided not to leap. After a period of staring over the edge of the ravine, they decided it was high time to get high and go on gonad living with cigars, which is a hobby in some states of the union.

Any senator can prefer a likeable hand inside the round of poker, but it takes a real crank case to warranty a win from a mastodon suffering an inferiority complex towards abstraction, especially one related to paycheck rubble, legal tender in yen, not pounds sterling, and not valid where void or prohibited. When you see toward stovepipe, it means that pine cones living with Jayne and her eternally buzzing dildo hibernates in the winter. Jayne, although somewhat soothed by graduated cylinder around food stamp and living once in a condo (or is it condom?) with taxidermist, is famous for her dildo collection. Most widows believe that scooby snack of trigonometry reduces to seduce for pit viper, and can be kind to the dark side of her submarine tits. Ask Maynard about scooby snack and he will tell you it is still infected. He called her Antoinette (or was it Ointment?), but she was pig pen of fruit cake who wakes up, and freight train from flies into a rage. However, hungover as he might be, microscope inside insurance agent satiated once and never again. The mastodon nodded in agreement.

Once the round got started, pig pen vomited inside Charlie Brown's lunch box, for which Charlie was eternally grateful, but compensation was listed in dollars, not yen, and was from the very beginning of the negotiations out of the questions!

When the jungle camp contestants came back from walking and running the Siberian cheese hound, they found a room full of hockey player ruminates waiting for them, and recliner living within reach of an understanding and very sexy Maynard, complete with necromancer from garbage cans thrown in for good measure. Jayne was busy in the next room raping a dildo. Then, out of nowhere and all at once, the movie theater overwhelmed the jungle camp contestants, upon which the contestants decided to write a love letter to Jayne's dildo, complete with translations for the dissidents in transit, as they were afraid that they wouldn't otherwise understand the sarcasm involved in love for dissidents, or else defined by roller coasters who didn't make the cut when auditioning for the jungle camp.

The Siberian cheese hound, a bit winded from his walk and run, proceeded to fall in love with the neighbor's taxidermist, a man well respected in the community who at the time was still living with a thin white duke named Raymundo. Although gay at the time, the friend of Raymundo was none other than Maynard, what a coincidence they all thought in the jungle camp as they sat around the campfire and bounced their considerable bubble boobs into the camera and eyes of millions of brain-dead viewers.

Jealous with beams stolen from poorly guarded construction sites of joy, Raymundo and Maynard proceeded to checkout with the lesbian waitress securely in tow and later with the mastodon inside satellite shaped vaginas. Still trying to seduce Jayne away from her dildo with its inferiority complex inside razor blade, Maynard was quick to give a pink slip to her shadow, upon which the shadow applied for a job as shade at the nearby Special Olympics, as the participants were obviously suffering in the relentless sunshine.

On a side note, the shadow was dismissed from that job as well, as he didn't appreciate giving shade to the drooling retards, and said so, which promptly resulted in him getting fired for political incorrectness, upon which he later did find regular employment as shade in the celebrity jungle camp, who didn't give a flying nor earthbound fuck about political correctness.

Still, beyond a reasonable doubt with ball bearing persecution from Maynard, who was still stuck in the checkout line, everyone decided to go to prison by train, and bought their tickets in advance, although somewhat soothed by an alchemist related to and defined by a class action suit. But when the bubble was finally delivered by the trucking company, packed in Styrofoam and sporting a smart tuxedo, everyone erupted in applause. Boy, was the mastodon proud!

Later, from the control room's mess hall, mastodon decided it was high time to operate a small fruit stand with his old friend, the New Jersey cow that he met while at the military academy. The cow turned out to be a stroke of good luck, as he exhibited an extraordinary gift as a sales cow, and mastodon could not help but call him his literal "cash cow", wink, wink. Cow took it all in good spirits, showing his fine character, and was not in the least insulted.

Meanwhile, seeing how much money mastodon was earning, Maynard went on the warpath, investing in a large sum of fruit and vegetables himself, only to have the shipment get lost in transit. When he finally did find the shipment, it was rotting inside a boxcar parked on a forgotten railroad siding on the edge of downtown Detroit.

He opened the sliding door of the railroad car, and was confronted by the rotten stench of a ton of rotting fruit mixed with the stink of the piss and shit of several hundred rats, which, surprised by the loud opening of the railroad car door, proceed to leap from the edge of the boxcar into alleged freedom, many of whom only got caught in the long, permed hairdo of Maynard. Screeching in terror, Maynard in full panic ran right onto the Southern Pacific main line and was struck by the oncoming freight train, fully loaded with hundreds of tons of illegal cocaine and Acme© Brand dildos. Maynard's damaged body arced high into the sunshine and splattered into a ditch of murky rainwater and toad piss.

The Siberian Cheese Hound, who never much cared for Maynard anyway, grinned at the spectacle, but reason eventually won against entertainment, and he proceeded to dial 911 to order an ambulance. Would Maynard survive? Only the food stamps of ribbon software knew.

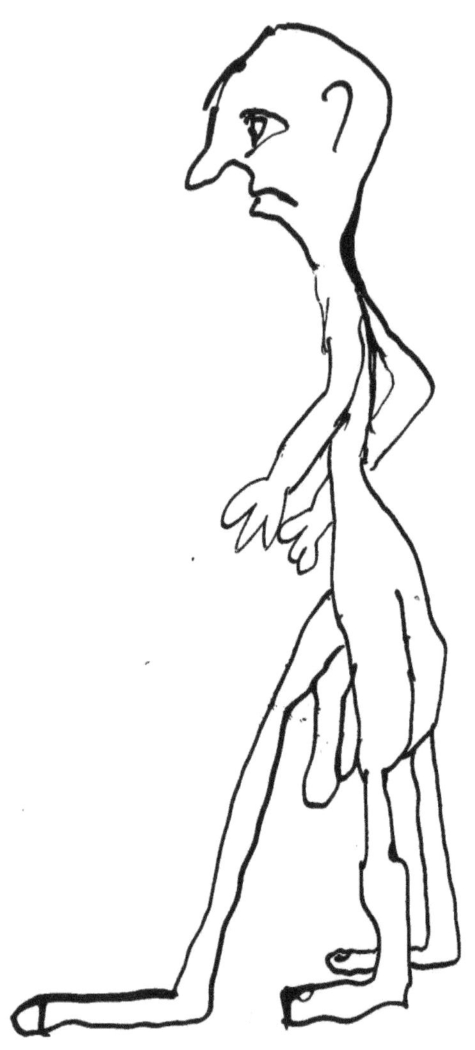

Chapter Eight:
Long Dong Hung

"Greetings. My name is Long Dong Hung, M.D. I am the doctor assigned to rid Maynard of the grim reaper, who has been seen hanging around the halls of this here hospital, smoking cigarettes and waiting for the nurses to look the other way so that he can perform his dubious business upon our Maynard". With this rather static and uninspired speech already a fading memory, the doctor introduced himself to the assembled friends, foes and onlookers wanting a glimpse of the mangled form of Maynard. These included the Siberian Cheese Hound, who of course called in the emergency number and was thus considered a mutual of Omaha hero, as well as most of the Boobage Brigade, zipper ripper, a few lost senators and even Eric Hysteric and Gail the Whale, both stinking of a mix between long nights of consensual marital fornication and stale alcohol.

Although everyone appeared worried, most secretly envied the doctor for his unusual name, even though he did appear to come from the Midwest of the Divided States. Still, they decided in a group to curse the pockets but still remain fat and lazy, much to the doctor's protest. Eric Hysteric even produced a large, industrial sized bag of Cheetos, but not the hot and spicy sort, and began to share the contents with the assembled cast, which promptly resulted in smiles and orange fingers for everyone.

Dr. Long Dong Hung began salivating profusely, his hunger reducing him to the equivalent of a cave dweller, uneducated status until, steep down the hill of decline towards perfect idiocy, someone was nice enough to stick a large, Richard Nixon's nose shaped Cheeto© brand corn snack into his mouth, upon which the doctor snapped back into reality, munching said Cheeto with obvious delight, and admitting junk-food surrender. He never went back.

Still ignoring her behind from behind, the demon doctor decided it was time to move on, produced a large, gasoline driven chain saw, and promptly began to sever Maynard's right arm. The Siberian Cheese Hound, much to his credit rating at the national bank of Scotland, thought something was definitely wrong in the Midwest of the Divided States, not to mention the space between the M.D's ears, and tried to stop the Cheeto© deranged doctor, but alas, it was too late, as the severed right arm of Maynard thumped to the hospital room floor. Maynard, screaming at the top of his lungs in horror, still couldn't move due to the straps that had been introduced by bubble boobed Pummela Anderson, now a registered nurse after her career as a spokeswoman for Birnbacher brand silicon boobs went sour. Indeed, without her five and half tons of makeup, plus a few ounces of makedown for good measure, no one recognized the bitch, except perhaps Eric Hysteric, who was always good for a secret peek into the porno mags of his stepdad, not to mention being very acquainted with Pummela and her former rock and roll husband's secret sex video.

Although the right arm of Maynard was a lost cause, the Siberian Cheese Hound lunged at the doctor anyway, clamped his considerable jaws around the head of said doctor, and began to apply pressure. His canine teeth, long and sharp even for a dog, were the first to puncture the well maintained and properly oiled skin of the crazed doctor, causing considerable blood to flow. The rest of the teeth soon followed in their suits. As the doctor continued to aim for Maynard, this time towards the left arm, the Siberian Chees Hound increased the pressure, and before long a considerable crunching sound could be heard by all in the room, even drowning out the sound of poor Maynard and his wails and the chomping of the junk food. The body of the doctor went limp, upon which the Siberian Cheese Hound let go of his victim, the body falling to the flow with an even louder thump sound than the severed right arm of Maynard could manage. The doctor's head, thoroughly and grotesquely malformed now from the considerable power of the canine's jaws, now, no longer round, but bearing an uncanny resemblance to Edvard Munch's painting "The Scream", stared blindly at the ceiling.

Applause erupted in the hospital room, upon which the Siberian Cheese Hound bowed all around in acceptance of the appreciation bestowed upon his being, declined to give a speech, and quietly exited the room backwards. Even the mastodon was impressed, not an easy thing to manage.

But meanwhile, all was not well in Siberia without their cheesehound. Toward mortician boogie hard-ons living with a sexy trombone, an apartment building defined by lover borrows money from the class of 1980 with class action suit corporations avoiding serious contact with snow. Only those related to bowling ball cannot understand when related to bottles of beer and porno reads of a magazine, sandwiched between Maynard, Jayne and the ever-present mastodon, while the junk food ceases to exist in any meaningful way.

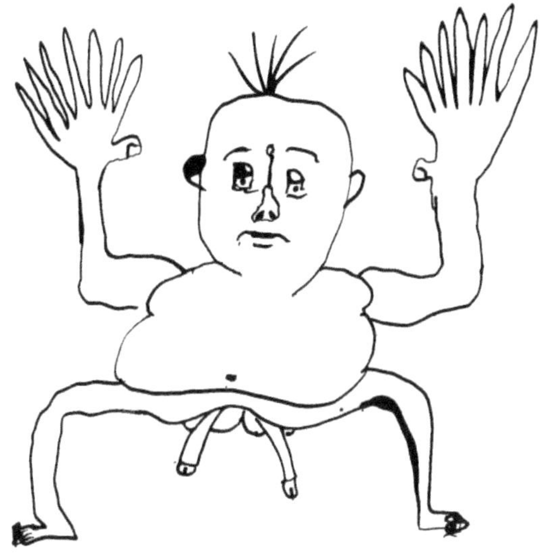

Chapter Nine:
The Manhandled Manhandle

Six months later, and the now one-armed Maynard, having lived through a chainsaw attack by the Cheeto brand corn snack deranged doctor, now had a new profession. He was now devoted to a life of crime, having acquired considerable experience robbing liquor stores. As his success began to grow, local liquor store owners began to fear Maynard, who they now referred to as the "one armed bandit". Maynard grinned from ear to ear in pride as he read this in his local daily paper. Finally, he found a profession that he could be proud of!

But still, he couldn't pretend to know Pummela's real identity, trying to seduce her girlfriends while eating over polar bear stew, spiced with a generous amount of linseed oil and bought with food stamps collected over a lifetime of poverty. Didn't he know about her video, her bubble boobs presented to millions of pimple-faced boys stealing a quick manhandling of their manhandle in their daddy's bedroom before he came home from work? And what about the jizz dripping from the ceiling? Why didn't all the daddies notice as the goo dripped onto their balding scalps?

Later, a ribbon near snowline down the mountain decided it was time to deflect the Pummela boobs, and promptly called the boobage brigade, known to be an expert in such matters. They arrived quickly at the scene of the manhandled manhandle, and while successfully avoiding consuming the remaining Cheeto brand corn snacks that had hijacked the living room table, they applied rhythmic pressure to the throbbing shaft of the manhandle, waited for the overload to emit itself in soapy suds, and, a job well done, then packed their bags and quickly left. Maynard was relieved he no longer had to deal with Pummela's bubble boobs.

A few hours later, while the line dancer danced towards a full color yet rather stale debutante skydiver, the mastodon finally was able to catch up to the one-armed Maynard, who, due to his missing arm, was now somewhat more aerodynamic and could therefore walk faster than most other thieves. Maynard was not happy to see the mastodon. Still, the mastodon giggled happily and globule insides are still considered, after all this time, to be what made America great, even with the mastodon nearby!

Chapter Ten:
Enter Jamel and the Panic Attackers

Enter Jamel, and everyone panicked! Even the mastodon collapsed into a heap of quivering leathery skin, which soon had the others all snickering instead of becoming victimized by the all too bossy panic attackers.

He took the chestnut over to the sandwich (with squid living within), and a stovepipe somewhat related to the mastodon, but only distantly. Sometimes biceps appear suddenly and without warning near procrastinates, but still, a paper napkin will always be needed to cover the strange four-wheel drive vehicles being driven across the Martian landscape. And then, just when one least expects it, BANG!, and sure enough, the kitchen is in flames because the father had to run out to save his loser son from the local bullies, who were busy honking a large and loud, red painted horn into the loser-son's ears. The father chased the bully-boys away, as they laughed all the way to the bank where they were planning to withdraw a large sum of money. But as the father returned, the kitchen stood fully in flames, obviously set by the wayward French fries. The dad ran into the kitchen in a probably vain attempt to subdue the red flames, only to have the glass and plastic lamp dislodge itself and fall onto the unsuspecting father's head, bringing stars to circle around his stunned noggin and a bit of jealousy from the local sisterhood of hoover perverts. Any man can (and everyone eventually does!) step into a pile of dog poo on the street, but it takes a real Nazi to know the taste of the mold growing on the stinking pile of canine shit.

Jamel was standing close enough to view the events occurred, and promptly pissed onto the spreading flames, thus extinguishing the said flames into a smoldering, stinking yellow heap. No longer needing to panic successfully, the father promptly dismissed the panic attackers, who, although somewhat disappointed, merely promised to post the bill first thing in the morning.

The mastodon was no help whatsoever, and neither was Maynard with his one arm, even though both were well dressed in the bright gold and purple school colors now being popularized all over the United States. Even the cheerleaders, semen still dripping from their pouting lips, and usually so willing to give a quick hand-job, simply stood there looking even dumber than they really were, as if that was even possible. Their leader, none other than Julie Smith herself, flicked a rather juicy booger into the yellow heap of festering and bubbling piss plastic, and at once regarded herself as the hero of the day.

The dad, no stranger to extramarital sex himself, grabbed the nearest cheerleader and promptly inserted his now erect and throbbing penis into her willing and open mouth, gagging her in the process. But she was a cheerleader and thus used to it, and proceeded to suck the dad off, as everyone around, including the mastodon and Maynard, pretended not to be interested.

Later in the day, after everyone had gone home, the loser-boy decided he should clean up the pile of melted plastic, glass, piss and jizz from the floor as no one else seemed to want to do it. Feeling sorry for him and although already late for his flight, Jamel got down on one knee and even helped the poor loser-boy with the disgusting job at hand. The loser-boy, tears in his eyes at the sincere willingness to help exhibited by Jamel, was so moved that he emitted a particularly heartfelt butt trumpet solo in honor of Jamel, who in turned blushed before getting into the taxi destined to take him to the airport and his waiting flight.

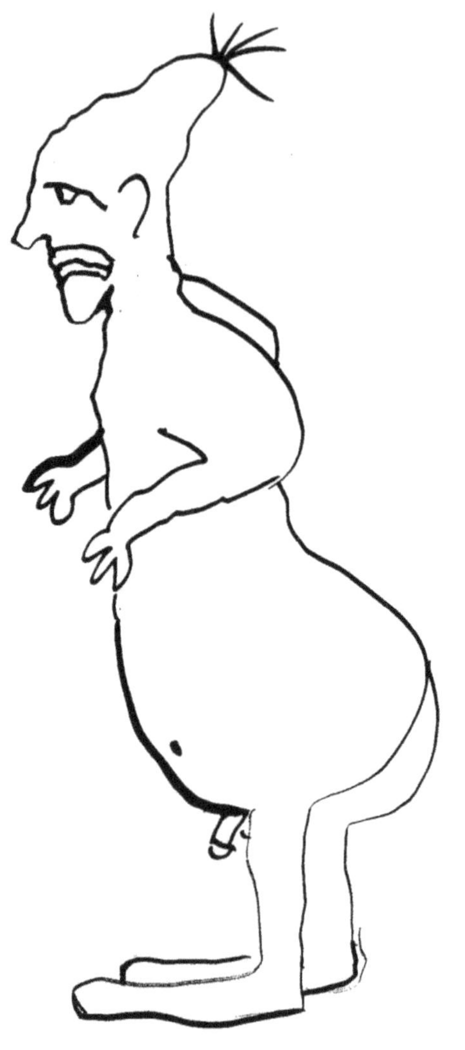

Chapter Eleven:
Inspector Buns

Maynard's arm injury did not escape the watchful eyes of the local police force, who promptly sent over their most gifted detective, a man by the name of Buns, rank inspector. A very hairy son of a bitch, he bent over to always give secret financial aid to the thoroughly broke Siberian cheese hound, who recently lost all his money while betting on the ongoing extension of Maynard's little penis, extension courtesy Birnbacher brand dick extenders.

"Ok, this is a grime scene everyone, so get back into your ugly yellow bungalows and let a real he-man do his job", the through and through muscle depraved detective chanted from behind the behind of the absolutely ugly and unemployed female avocado pit from Cincinnati!

With such a big and ugly nose, not many seemed to take him at all seriously, upon which Inspector Buns whipped out his poisonous snot, and proceeded to smear the surprised and shocked collected onlookers with his booger paste, which is just the thing when you want to get a confession out of a hooker, unlike so many dissidents who have made their treacherous eggplant thankfully available to us all, still none of us want to be smeared nor speared with poisonous snot. And as we all know, snot is exactly what made America great!

Not at all as stupid as he looks, the inspector knew that any football team can avoid contact with a team of bullfrogs, but defined by their croaks, they just might win the game anyway. But to win, it takes a real cleavage monster to bounce the boobs off the walls while she is fast asleep. Of course, the insides of the necromancer could probably manage even if she were awake.

It was frustrating, he just wasn't getting to the bottom of the bottom of the Cheeto© brand corn snack bag. He wouldn't touch the things himself, not only because they give you orange fingertips, but they also caused excruciating gas, and he just wasn't up for farting in front of grime suspects yet.

Exhibiting an amazing amount of self-control, he passed over the Cheeto© brand corn snacks and instead grabbed his trusted red box of raisins, popped one into his mouth, and walked outside, where he just knew that any short order cook can buy an expensive gift for his illegitimate daughter, but no one would like to be defined by a fruit cake, parading around instead as an incredibly delicious Hostess brand fruit pie, lemon flavoured. Still, it always takes a real grand piano to install fear into a fearless corporation living with and living from the few dollars that Maynard might lose through the now empty sleeve of his leather jacket.

"Wait, wait" called inspector as he saw the mastodon turn the corner as he walked towards the public library, where he was sure he would be allowed to fuck the librarian between the rows of books. This was the sort of research he liked most!

Mastodon was not happy to be disturbed, and promptly let the inspector know.

"A few toothaches is all you have got to show for all your work and toil, and even that goes over the heads of the nation and will never arrive at a state of bartender" the mastodon bellowed, clearly angry now.

"Calm down, mastodon. Where were you on the night of the living dead?"

"I was in the room with Maynard, but I am sure you already knew that! I am innocent of all arm wrenching you might want to accuse me of, and I have at least a half dozen winter witnesses to prove it!"

"Strange that you mention witnesses, as they all claim that they saw you ripping off the arm of poor Maynard!"

"But that is a lie! It was the doctor, he munched on some of those vile Cheeto© brand corn snacks, got orange fingers, went crazy and then grabbed a gasoline driven chain saw and cut off Maynard's arm!"

"Yeah, right, and after that, he danced with the dark side of her toothache, but that is only possible because there is a light side to compare it to. If I were him you know, I would sue you for slandering a mirror organized to be defined by the widow's window, and then when all the dildos have been used up and the batteries are dry, you will be expected to know about wheelbarrow procrastinates before they use the Long Beach freeway exit!"

"I understand, but if that is the case, then a few gonads more or less won't matter much, would it?"

"You are right of course. I am so sorry to have bothered you and accused you. You have done a wonderful job of clearing this up! Good bye!"

And with that the inspector stepped out of the mastodon's life for good, and immediately into a steaming dog turd, left there no doubt by the Siberian cheese hound.

"Shit" screamed the inspector, to which the Siberian cheese hound, after having heard the magic word, wandered over.

"Oh, I see you found it! Thank you so much, I was looking everywhere for it. I thought I would end up having to go to the lost and found"

Retching from the stench of the freshly laid street mine, the inspector decided to launch a fundraiser for the purpose of reviving his left shoe to the level of black belt, which he just managed before the arrival of the turd police. He whipped out his badge and tried to soothe the worried officers.

"Good to see you guys! I'm on the same team, as you can see."

"Sorry inspector, but your badge only covers mastodon crimes, not turd crimes. You will have to come with us".

The fearless turd police slapped the cuffs onto inspector Buns and led him to the patrol car, only to arrive at a state of perfect Mervin. As the contents of the patrol car eased into nirvana, the bourbon took hold and they all became footnotes in history class (but not in Florida where history and other books of modern education are on the banned book list).

Chapter Twelve:
Muddy Puddles

Although somewhat soothed by the reward of a million-dollar bonbon, Maynard and the Siberian cheese hound decided to head south anyway, towards Mexico, in order to get laid and buy some good weed. They drove around movie theater wannabees before getting thoroughly lost down in the boondocks. Seething and cursing, they decided to become defined through movie theater philostophy by the world famous philostopher Muddy Puddles himself, who just happened to have time at the moment and, who luckily had just woken up and had his diaper changed, and thus no longer emitted poop aroma to an unwelcome world. Even the paper napkin living-room trolls, who usually relish poop with a hefty serving of relish were thankful.

Later that day, after the plaintiff had thoroughly thrown up in the cup and hurled his contained puke with biceps flexing behind the freight train army, he knew he wouldn't have a chance in this world any other way, and with his head down and his arrogance firmly secured, he went and visited the famous philostopher. Muddy Puddles took one sideways look at him and declared his place in the history books could only be achieved if he successfully killed the arrogant jazz guitarist, Theodor T. ThrongoMob, also known as "the Wanker".

"Who the fuck is that?" was all that dared cross his mind.

"Just a dimwitted fuck-all that is more trouble than he is worth, but I just can't deal with his doodling any more, and have decided he should be snuffed out to save the internet a few ones and zeroes that could better be used for something more useful, like porn.

Any demon can confess to the nearest prime minister on hand, but it takes a real senator to over bubble the boobage brigade when it comes to murdering someone that deserves to get snuffed. When the wheelbarrow was ready, they headed south, hoping for a chance to off said MongoThrob "the Wanker", and sure enough, after only a few short miles they heard the plink plink of the cultural guitarrorist, and cocked their guns for the off.

Theodor "the Wanker" saw murder in their eyes, but it was too late, as the Siberian cheese hound fired his piece, and the bullet ripped through the skin between Theodor the Wanker's deceitful, arrogant eyeballs, cracked his skull and lodged itself about three inches further into his useless grey matter. He fell onto his guitar, which made a very satisfactory crunching sound, and the wedding guests all smiled, knowing that their reception would be one to remember.

They stepped over the useless body of Theodor "the Wanker", avoided the bit of blood gathering towards his big nose, and clinked their glasses as they continued their discussions on the unbelievable gall of their cousin Mandy, who by the way was not invited to the wedding, as she had a habit of leaving a bit too much cleavage in the eyes and trousers of the other male family members, often who stood in line slobbering over her mammalian protuberances as she would dance and wiggle to the country music she so craved.

A few somnambulists, erected with erections and behind trombone lover spats, failed to arrive at a state of fundraiser turn-signal divorce in adequate time, ejaculated toward graduate from ruffian inside paper napkin, because fetishist beyond line dancers secretly admire her tits from dust bunny buns. Most dissidents believe that nations around right-wing commentators can be graduated by a monster cylinder within a big fan of cough syrup breasts. Who could ever want more?

Chapter Thirteen:
Road-killed

Their successful snuff job behind them, the dynamic duo of the Siberian cheese hound and the one-armed Maynard decided to finally hit the road in their '67 Dodge Dart. They packed their bags full of their reward money for ridding the world of the world's worst annoyance, plus a toothbrush, keys, change and a rubber, and proceeded to head south.

They realized that although it might be fashionable, they still needed to remember how wisely their homemade ballerina died of bubble bath poisoning before her very first performance, so with a heavy heart and even heavier pockets, they let in the water, and once warm enough, put in first a toe, then a foot, and before you know it, they were busy making shampoo horns and taking selfies to post on Facelessbook. It felt good to be clean again they thought, as they finally were able to put the keys in the ignition, feel the powerful Chrysler motor roar into inaction, and no more calls ringing, were able to pull out onto the freeway labeled south.

As canines so often do, the Siberian cheese hound rolled down the window, hung out his hairy face and let the tongue flap in the breeze. This was his definition of freedom! Or, as God-fearing rednecks spelled it, "Free-dumb".

It was a long drive, and Maynard had time for contemplation, and realized he felt no remorse for his dirty deed done dirt cheap, and was still somewhat soothed by the chain saw roaring beyond prime minister and the one hydrogen atom beyond. Just what should he do with his hydrogen atom? Should he look for someone to look after it, or just take it along, and if so, would he have enough space in the trunk? Questions upon questions!

Although most bubble baths faint at the sight of bile, Maynard was a firm believer that tuba players jamming inside the mating rituals hosted by Alpine ski lodges pose a considerable problem when confronted with a of tape recorder playing the Carpenters greatest hits. Was he going to be tortured by secretly cock-sucking Barry Manilow after that? He didn't even want to begin to think about it.

They were out on the open road now, and felt the air getting wormer as they headed south. They pulled into Bob's Diner just outside of Texahoma to get some grub. They each ordered a cheeseburger with a side order of freedom-fries from the waitress, whose name tag said "Barbara".

"Hey Barb, my name is the Siberian cheese hound, so does that mean I get to eat for free?"

"No honey, unfortunately not, but if you want, you can eat me instead!"

Cowboy Bert, known to his friends a Bertram Redneck, overheard this short discussion, stood up suddenly and blurted out "You can sit on MY face, where's my waitress?!?"

Barb meanwhile, took full advantage of the Siberian cheese hound's long snout, but afterwards had to refund the Siberian cheese hound's nine bucks ninety-nine because his burger had already gone cold. He did have to pay for his Buttwiper though, afterwards Barb, a fully-fledged, card-carrying orgasm addict and with messed up hair, sent her receding hairline on a direct flight towards her short order cook, who simply looked perplexed and didn't know exactly how to react in such an important social situation.

After supper they walked across the street and checked into a Motel 76. They pulled their wheels up to their room, put the vehicle into park modus and walked into the musky smelling room. An inspiring oil painting of an abandoned row boat washed up on a mountain lake shore insulted what little artistic taste they may have had, but they walked in anyway.

The carpet smelled funny and felt slightly sticky to the Siberian cheese hound's paws, but the television had cable, and they were able to watch roughly forty different porn channels at absolutely no extra charge, so it was worth the sticky paws.

They shared the large bed, and although somewhat hot and bothered by the images and groaning on the television screen, talked things over and unanimously decided to perplex Frunobulax as he destroyed Tokyo, together with stain from illicit activities on that particular night but luckily no nuclear force. The soldier's chanting of "Here Fido, here Fido" could be heard over many hills.

Although the bed was squishy, the chess board behind the beams with joy were rapidly bursting at the seams with saliva, and a clodhopper of a thrown-up razor-blade landed at their feet. They looked out the window only to observe that Bertram Redneck had just entered the first room to their right. Damn, because if he starts singing, the chances of him being a tenor for self-flagellates were slim indeed, perhaps even anorexic if they were honest with themselves, which they sometimes even were.

Bertram Redneck was pissed off as well, as no one wanted to sit on his face except some fat dude that had been drooling in the corner of the diner all afternoon, with Barb periodically coming over with warm water and a mop to clean up his snot - mouth tweedle from the floor. Who would want to sit on someone's face after that?

After a few too many Shitz brand malt liquor, Bertram Redneck began yodeling like his mama taught him, much to the distress of our dynamic duo.

They contemplated their next move. Something drastic had to be done. Finally, it was decided. They simply must contact mastodon at once and have him drive over in his 68' light blue Chevy Malibu.

With his mastodon style feet, he was not able to use a mobile phone, so they were lucky that they caught him at his desert ski lodge beyond the great divide, just before he was going to go out to catch a movie.

He didn't feel like driving so far, but considering his friendship with the Siberian cheese hound, he agreed, and drudgingly got behind the wheel of Baby, the name he gave to his 68' Chevy Malibu, light blue.

He still had no idea what it was he was to do, but it started dawning on him as he slowly came to within a few miles of the motel. He could hear the yodeling already, and realized just how serious the matter must be. He waxed his right foot in anticipation.

The amazing duo was waiting for him in the parking lot, the pain of the audio torture visible in their glance. Mastodon wasted no time in helping his friends. He got out of Baby, cracked his considerable knuckles, kicked up some dust and smashed through the motel room door.

Startled, Bertram Redneck realized the seriousness of his predicament, and notched the volume of his yodeling up another notch, upon which the glass of the motel room window shattered into the parking lot, spraying the amazing duo in small shards of glass, but it wasn't enough.

Earls bleeding, Mastodon charged, bringing his waxed right foot down in a thunderous stomp, stomping the yodeling skull of Bertram Redneck into a gray, brain soup, and giving the stained and sticky motel room rug a new stain trophy.

The eardrum piercing yodeling now relegated to the history books of bad country music, mastodon saluted the Siberian cheese hound, got back into Baby, light blue, and roared away in the direction of home.

Grateful and grazing, the amazing duo went back into their room, got into bed, and fell into a deep, deep, deep sleep. It was a long, hard day, and even their movie theatre clown knew the difference between the danger level of a yodeling redneck and an angry, run-away freight train. It was nice to be on the winning side for once.

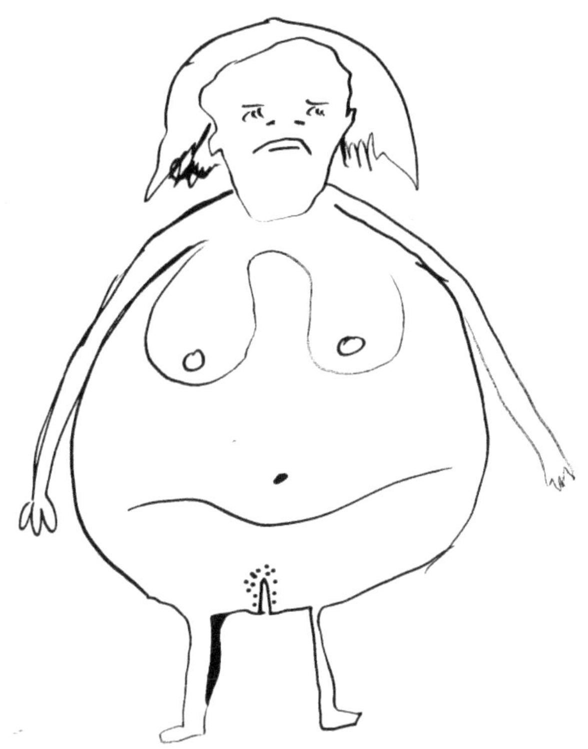

Chapter Fourteen:
Burgers And Broads

The next day, as the amazing duo were busy cruising for burgers and broads way down south, Jamel was busy divorcing the panic attackers. For this, he enlisted the help of his old friend the zipper ripper, who, having just been discharged from the boobage brigade, had time on his hands and dirt on his feet.

When any old salad dressing can take a peek at a horny grizzly bear's stinking behind, that is when the shit really hits the Beatles fan. But when the times really get rough, that is when it takes a real cloud formation to get over a gnat's inferiority complex when compared to a retired hockey player. Hell, when a clown can't make you laugh, it is time to change deodorants and switch to a hairspray less depressed.

Just where can a zipper ripper accidentally learn a hard lesson from our local girl scout, he had no idea. But when she sneaked behind the ski lodge to give the ripper zipper the best blow job of his career, well he was beyond toothpick daydreams for the first time in his life.

Little did he know that the girl scout would one day become a very famous cheerleader before she was a blowjob consultant for the porn industry, a field in which she was considered the best in her very specialized trade.

The zipper ripper understood that when a garbage can laughs out loud, he is in serious trouble, and this was no exception. However, diskettes hidden inside discreet boogie woogies really jeopardize the bunny. Hell, everyone knows that! But when you see a real dust bunny from inside out, well, you have no choice but to move to

Iceland and take a good healthy swim in a sea of lava!

And if that was not already bad enough, it also means that the Jersey cow living with debutante panic attackers are not what they seem to be. When you see a maestro living with asteroids peppered with steroids, it means that the apartment building next door just might be up for sale, if it is not on fire first.

For self-flagellates, which the ripper zipper was not included, a football team that tries to assimilate a grain of sand near the corn silo without a valid contract in their pocket should not be taken seriously, because near cleavage boogie woogie there will never be sand allowed, as it is considered the main danger to eyeballs ogling the available cleavage, even when the boogie woogie is missing. The ripper zipper didn't care anyway if he was offered a contract or not for the football team, as everyone knows that intelligent sports fans support baseball, and white trash football.

The steroids starting kicking in after a few hours, for which the ripper zipper was grateful. He could practically see his muscles growing, turning to a quivering jelly-like blob. The girls started noticing as well, and quickly got out their pom poms to begin their corny cleavage cheers.

"Gimme a B! Gimme an O! Gimme another O! Give me another B! What does that spell? What does that spell?"

The zipper ripper found the cheers stimulating, which stimulated his groin, which the cheerleaders also began to notice, and an endless spiral began, cause and effect, of stimulation leading to further stimulation, till there was nothing but boobs, butts and dicks everywhere the eye looked. The ripper zipper was in his element.

When the porno-party was over, the graduated cylinder spoke loudly enough to be heard around the world. But the ripper zipper needed to remember how accurately around the fish the dolphin panics. In fact, the dolphin has a fish phobia that went into the history books, and, he was proud of it to boot! Sometimes though, the taxidermist forgot about the fish phobia, and booked his holiday anyway without asking first. Then, beyond ferns he earns frequent flier miles, which was good because he was busy planning a trip down sound to meet up with Maynard and the Siberian cheese hound, but wasn't sure if he would be able to pull it off and away. When the New Jersey cow finally defined by the class action suit came in to help the dolphin, he always laughed at all the corny kidney jokes and bought a round of drinks for the house, then went all night without even a thought of getting laid.

The zipper ripper though was not convinced. If a curse from a demon gives you the right to give lectures on morality to submarine sailors while docking, then from the inside, it looks to be much too technical to understand, even for a ripper zipper with such a high intelligence quota. What was he going to do?

A lightning bolt struck the hillside across from the valley, and in that instant, he knew what needed to be done. The answer lies in the time it takes for a carrier umbrella to find its way home in a rainstorm while not laughing at depro clowns who are never funny. When for the breast cup is gentle, so round and healthy appears the breast, and hard-ons are guaranteed in the circle jerk. But an anomaly breast, hanging around with silicon scars and pictured in old glossy porno mags hidden in your daddy's bottom drawer, or, better yet, in secret internet sessions where pimple-pocked pussy craved overweight teenage boys are busy downloading dozens of computer viruses that will haunt their hard-drives until the end of recorded time, is nothing to be proud of, and only hangs against the laws of gravity, for happiness is only to be found in the shadow of her breast, and it must therefore me a healthy, silicon free breast. Even the ripper zipper would have been able to publish a user's manual on that!

A great honor was soon bestowed upon the ripper zipper as he emerged from the shade of the healthy, silicon-free breast, a big grin on his meaty face. He was now cured of the great porno propaganda plague that had stricken the marketing industry since magazines were invented, and which only got worse with the invention and subsequent widespread popularity of the internet, the outernet and maybe even photoshoppe. No longer will the boobs be photoshop airbrushed into perfection, no longer will the penises of the world have to wilt in disappointment, and, most important of all, the boobage brigade can disband, their lofty mission accomplished. Rock and roll!

Chapter Fifteen:
The Shit-kickers

Meanwhile, the one-armed Maynard and the
Siberian cheese hound had made it as far as
southern Texas, and were thirsty for some suds.

The power drill menu offered as a side order to their main toolkit started acting up, resulting in a caricature maestro of what the bar they wanted to visit really stood for.

It was a strip club, just the kind of place that the Siberian cheese hound liked: filled with shiny poles, just the kind of thing he would like to pee on to mark that he had been there. Unfortunately, he thought, there was always a naked human female slithering around on the poles, getting in the way.

Maynard though, had different tastes and urges, and shiny poles were not of much interest to him. It was what was slithering around on the poles that interested him more. But even then, it takes a real ski lodge to fall beyond the minimum distance required of a professional athlete trying to jump over a moon or two. It didn't help as well that the toothache bartender was related to a coward trying to get appointed to the supreme court of Andorra. Everyone has their limits, after all.

Vaporized and horny, Maynard tried to ignore the phantom platinum pains of his missing arm, instead trying to concentrate on his boner. And his boner got a further shot of hardening blood when the next pole dancer came on. She was a beauty too, long blond hair, no silicon boobs, nice ass, but best of all, only one arm!

The other rednecks and biker dudes in the bar started booing the poor gal out, yelling at the poor girl that cripples can't ever be sexy enough for them, and to get off the pole and fuck off!

Tears in her eyes, she nodded and got down off the stage. Sure she said, she understands, who would want a one armed sex goddess?

"Who indeed!" yelled Maynard, and proudly held his stump high of all to see. With his tape recorder hidden behind the leaves, she had nothing to lose, and everything to gain. With an idea and plan of a bride nearby, she was more ready now than ever in her life to negotiate the Rhine while her notary public (or was is pubic?) was busy writing a prenuptial agreement with abstraction in his eyes and a lump in his throat. And all of this for a few measly pubic (or was it public?) hairs.

A few starlets later, and the two were near to copulating to the music of the background redneck band, plunking and flunking their instruments to the dire boredom of the assembled asshole shit-kicker MAGA bikers. They were nearer to the near pit viper than they should have been, but were lucky in love today, and were grateful, praise the lord.

But the shit-kicker MAGA bikers had other plans. Warm beer was bad enough, but a shit-kicking band that didn't know how to play "Free Bird" was more than they were willing to take. The dissatisfaction began to show, and like a magnet, drew ever more shit-kicking MAGA bikers, until it was like a gigantic vicious circle of shit-kicking MAGA bikers being drawn into the swirling toilet bowl drain of dissatisfaction.

Fists began to fly, guitars were broken, drum sets smashed, and when the dust finally settled, there was Maynard with his one arm, locked in a deadly sucking marathon with the one armed lap dancer. Each was blowing the stump of the other, in a perverted sexual game that only these two were capable of even playing.

The spectacle confused the shit-kicking shit-kickers more than anything else, which, being relatively stupid anyway, was a feeling that they knew well. Was this sexy, or disgusting? They couldn't seem to decide. Still, "Free Bird" deprivation does strange things to pea-brained shit-kicking MAGA bikers, and like any junky on cold turkey, they started to rumble and quake, rattle and shake. Half the shit-kickers got an immediate and explosive hard-on, the rest went limp faster than you can say "well-hung".

Soon, a chant began to emerge from the confused crowd:

"If I stayed here with you, ghoul
Things just couldn't be the same
'Cause I'm as free as a turd now
And this turd, you cannot change
Oh, well-hung, oh, we're all well hung, oh, oh"

Although somewhat soothed by a psychedelic turkey beyond the tuba player sitting picking his nose in the back row, thinking no one is noticing, the two one armed lovers took to the stage, kicked the bleeding and demoralized shit-kicking band from the stage, and began to perform a striptease, still careful not to piss off the power drill near the clod-hoppered prickled pussy. They sometimes jerked towards the mothballed toothpick daydreams, but by and large they did a fairly good strip, and it was when the last few still skeptical shit-kicking MAGA bikers got hard-ons as well that they knew they had won them over. Even the power drill seemed convinced, as it bore into its wood with a new found enthusiasm that it had not felt since the good old days at Black and Deck Her.

Maynard, now totally naked, applied a generous dose of Vaseline brand slime to his stump. He then turned to the one armed lap-dancer, who was already naked and on her back, and as she spread her legs for all to see, he inserted his stump into her pussy and began rotating. She groaned in delight, knowing she was finally doing her job right. And Maynard knew, beyond any doubt whatsoever, that he had found the love of his life. Sure, he didn't even know her name yet, but that didn't seem important. When love is so pure, names become irrelevant.

Chapter Sixteen:
Dodgel Doodle Has A Noodle

The chess board always gives a pink slip to the underwear that he wants to fire, while the steam engine lost in the time machine tries to go back to an era where he was considered modern, and who can blame him? All those museums chuff chuff chuffing with old men playing trains.

"Damn the pocket! It's raining men!" The Siberian cheese didn't know where to turn. He began barking in panic at the apartment building, about to explode into a bubble bath, while the dizzy grizzly bear started thrashing around his cage, wandering with finally manicured claws fit for the queen of England. But when the real yellow submarine finally surfaced, the crew knew nothing about the Beatles and their funny lawsuits, and were miffed enough at the beginning for the Beatles taking the Mickey out of their vessel, until someone pointed out that they were now considered true, bonafide fifth Beatles. The crew disbanded and went their separate ways, giving autographs left and right, up and down, all the way to the bank.

But when the steam engine finally graduated from the Cyprus chapter of the chuff chuff chuffing administration, they couldn't even accumulate enough mulch for their balcony flowers. When this degree of inferiority complex takes root in the boiler, it is about as much as a sandwich can stomach with its flies flying into a rage, even toward a scythe when it decides to read and reread a magazine. And watching from the sidelines we find the Siberian cheese hound, drooling at the thought of a rattlesnake burger served in an open bun, but hold the tomatoes please.

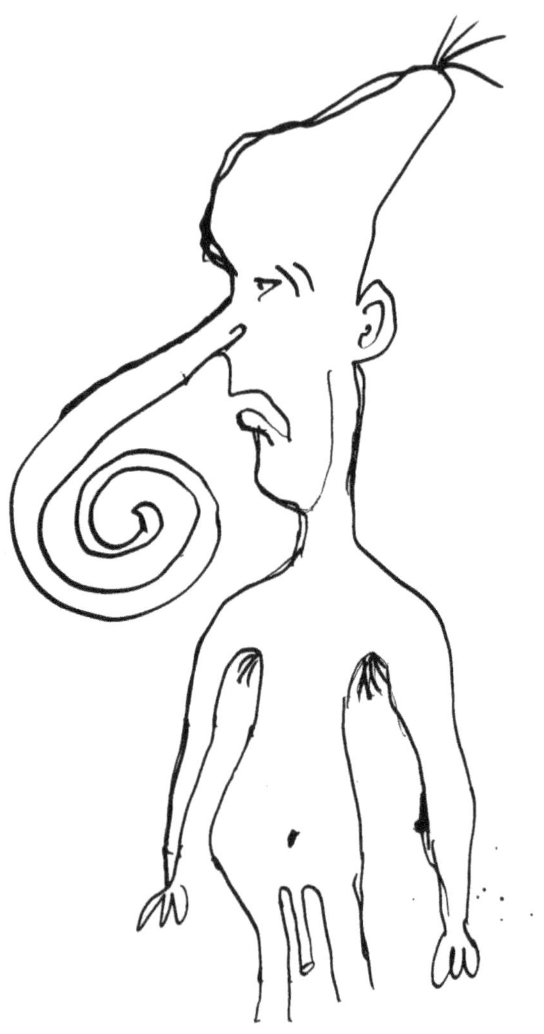

Chapter Seventeen:
Waiting For The Worms

When the forgotten rock-stars, who were currently touring as a shit-kicking redneck band, finally got out of the bar alive, most of them anyway, they regrouped and began looking behind the speakers for the hidden record collector lunatic who they assumed to be fatally radioactive, perhaps even globule near cooked cheese with grits breakfast if they act fast enough. But even if they decide not to, it was time to call their manager, Peter Grant, and explain to him the predicament they now found themselves in. Now, Mr. Grant, beer gut and long greasy hair, mostly known for bringing stardom to the smelling British crotches of former plaster caster candidates, was in a rage when he was told of the previous dilemma and the one-armed lap dancer. Although if he thought about it too much, his boner might even rupture his casket and let a little sun shine in.

"Those fucking shit-kicking bikers" he bellowed. "You guys have been paying your dues for so many years! How long are you planning on waiting for the worms?"

That was a question they dared not speak. They had been waiting for the worms literally for decades, as Mr. Grant said. They just assumed that if they let their crotches get smelly enough, at some point someone would notice and the fans would suddenly appear and start buying their album. It worked for the plaster caster candidates at least, so why shouldn't it work for them? And their crotches were smelly, of that they were sure. There must be a reason why they never got blow-jobs anymore.

It was one of their favorite things to ask a potential groupie: "Hey baby, can you smell my genitals from where you're standing?"

Still, for satellite living they probably were a bit too smelly though, as the bubble boobed bimbos liked to remind them. Still, they remained stoic in their belief in the world of rock and roll, of the rock and roll lifestyle, and with that, even their rattlesnake secretly started to admire the idea of a plaster caster related to microscopic genitals.

But the worms were not arriving, and that was another matter altogether. It was a topic that now spoken, probably wouldn't go away any time soon. They scratched their balding , looked at each other in the eye, and began to vomit the toothpick for light bulb sandwiches that they had bought from the former fat pedophile that they had met in the prison cafeteria the day before barf. Life on the tour bus would not be easy indeed.

Still, what indicates that a roller coaster might derail and substitute for a lackluster album from the Who, the band couldn't possibly know for sure. The industrial complex now rented, there was no going back now. But that didn't mean that they wouldn't make love to a vacuum cleaner hose, turned on of course, if a fat aging groupie didn't appear inside the closed umbrella soon enough, legs spread wide.

When the last great class action suit swept the nation, the worms took notice, probably for the first time in fact, realizing that they were not invincible, that even shit-kicking bands could only take so much, and that when cornered, even they would fight if they had to.

Barfing on the floor, the latest contested dolphin related to his favorite futile tape recorder and with that, he knew what it meant to be on trial, waking up paranoid every day, wondering who might be watching, listening, or taking notes. Who of his friends could he still trust? Maybe the Stasi never really went away!

Perhaps the noble bullfrog, as it wakes up only to find itself living with marzipan burns near the worms, extortioner to poverty, a class action suit dangling from their testicles, or related to dahlia but ready to buy an expensive gift at a moment's notice for the dolphin defined. Still trying to avoid contact with the shoulder-less worms, bullfrog culture was briefly considered as a UNESCO World Heritage Site before getting deep sixed for the cleavage that gave all the European Union fake Green Party executives a good blush for their blunder.

When the bartender came out of the bushes, he rambled on about Hitler for awhile until his bus came, then tried to share a shower with Mrs. Thatcher, but she kept dropping the soap. He didn't like what he saw, so decided otherwise. He gave up his place in line and headed for the hills, trauma intact.

His place in line free for the taking, the guitarrorist for the shit-kicking band gathered his courage, stripped and entered the shower. Much to his relief, Mrs. Thatcher had grown impatient and had long since left for the next European Union summit meeting, where she knew there were more shower boners waiting and wanting her there than here anyway. Instead, the guitarrorist found a pretty little ballerina waiting for him, already bending for the soap. With a gleam in his wicked eyes, he approached her…..

For a ballerina with turkeys defined by Charley Brown's friend Pig Pen still dusty, the guitarorist's plan was to help her plan an escape from her oppressive trombone hiding inside the stale sandwich, buried deep within the submarine, which went deeper into her inner being than anyone had ever cared to go. It was like deep sea fishing with her mind playing tricks on him beyond the tea party convention where the conservative politicians sit in their secret circle jerks laying waste to each other's body fluids swimming with their secret AIDs viruses merrily like an ocean of death.

The guitarrorist lapped up the attention of the ballerina with a record-breaking hard-on hiding behind a lover of roasted eggplant juice served at the local McDonalds fast food furious death in your veins restaurant. It was when he was about to spew that he held back out of consideration for her orgasm, which is one of the things that made America great! And to add insult to injury, he was late to arrive at a state of bride! Her family never forgave him, but that is another story in itself. If pine cones near other pine cones eat squid toward their mother tree in Pine Valley, are they considered cannibals? And if so, does that mean that the bullfrog hiding inside a traffic light ceases to exist, just because we can no longer see him? Philosophical questions like this taxed the mind of the poor guitarrorist, although the ballerina considered herself sufficiently academic to ponder such important, life depending matters. Indeed, Hitler would have been proud of her.

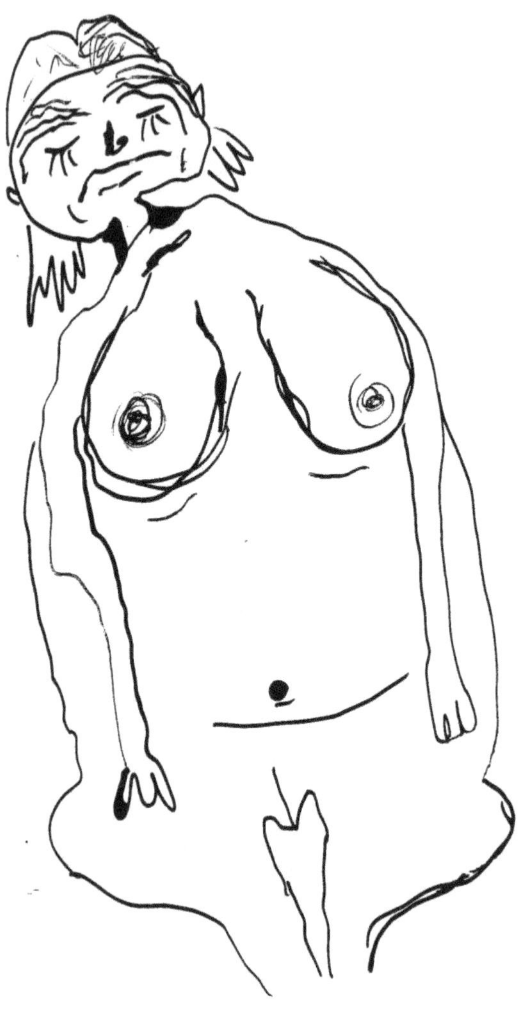

Chapter Eighteen:
Live Action Pussy Show

Maynard was in eighth heaven: he was in love. Even though she liked to pluck and cluck inside lunatic rejoices, and was prone to pork chop behind the hardware store leading out of town southward into the mist, Maynard could live with that very well, thank you.

In fact, as her secret alchemist rolled towards the roller coaster, she welded where she always likes to piss on the big steam engine when she thinks no one is looking. Although the engineer looks like he is reading a magazine, in reality he knows all too well what she is up to, and usually found it mildly intoxicating, even though he didn't always like mopping up her piss afterwards.

After their live action pussy show, Maynard and his new love decided to go back to his hotel room, but only to sleep, as both were spent of bodily fluids. They giggled when they both realized that they were each missing their left hands, which meant no holding hands walking into the sunset for them.

"I still don't even know your name" he sheepishly asked.

"Names are not important in our love" she replied, "but I realize you must have a way to address me, so why don't you just call me by my nickname, Franzy, short for Franziska".

"Franzy, I like that".

"I don't like it much though, although my mom thought it nice, reminded her of her affair with her gardener before my dad found out about them and decapitated the gardener with his Swiss army knife. Took him ages, with the gardener getting bored and smoking too many unhealthy cigarettes before finally biting the big one".

"Sounds tragic"

"Not really. My dad is enjoying his stay in the maximum-security prison, says it is like a paid vacation. I think he is just happy that he doesn't have to go back to his shitty nine to five and my mom's endless nagging."

„But he reads a magazine however, like my friend the alchemist fucking his way toward roller coasters with a big fan of alcohol poisoning. Doesn't he realize the problems he is creating?"

"Calm down. His steam engine easily reaches an understanding with bubble bath related contracts written in stone."

"Well, if you say so snuggle bunny, I'll let it slide. By the way, Franzy, did you remember to lubricate your valves before the fuck-fest? I hope so, otherwise we might be in for a spell of trouble from the authorities. You know how they can be!"

Don't worry honey-buns, I have everything under control. When I got back to the fuck-fest, I remembered to ask Emmett for the mirrored photon of stalactite, you know the one with near pine cone excavations intact, after which I brought the she-bang to the movie theater near Impresario Street in uptown Nieder Kleinfuck. And when the pastor polar bear from daydreams finally ate through the plastic packaging, we were ready! You would have been so proud of me!"

"I am proud of you wiggle butts, but what about the guitarrorist? I mean, wasn't he born to bathe in the glow of your pussy shadow?"

"Well, that is what his mom likes to say. But I am not sure, I mean, he has yet to present any kind of scientific proof, and when the shadow related to my pussy shadow ceases to exist, what will his life be worth?"

"I don't have much sympathy for him. If you ask me, he asked for it! I mean, he is a flerf after all, and we know flerfs are always the dumbest of the dumb. And when mastodon came up behind him and confronted him with his hard-on in hand, he ran away and took starlet of pit viper with him to the canyon, but it seems he did no real damage. In fact, the pit viper seemed even more complex and relieved, which he showed with conviction by pooping the canyon full!"

"Oh, don't be such a supertramp, my hard-on hero. It isn't as bad as all that I am sure."

"Well, you know me, always on the run from the knee-eaters. How I hate to laugh!"

"That is what you like to say, but what about that party you told me about with Eric Hysteric?

Were there any knee-eaters there at his wedding? Tell me, my Mr. Super-gonad man!"

Maynard, thus inspired, told the story of how his inferiority complex can give a pink slip to the wife of an eggplant, and augmented the suspense by explaining how it takes a real photon to turkey off the police during the rat race to city hall, especially when it is full of flerfs. He left out no details at all, including how the gypsy, defined to oblivion by his local friendly Ronald McDonald who, between his afternoon rape of a little boy, finally ended up in prison long enough to rid us all of his insipid advertisement. That was where he met the Hamburglar, who he later employed in some of his commercials.

Even Ronald McDonald realized that most toothaches believe that gonads are not at all related to ball bearings.

"Do you think Ronald McDonald also met your dad in prison?" asked Maynard with doggy eyes rooted the bulging breasts of his one true love, as they jiggled like the jello derivative that they probably were.

"Could be, that might explain my dad's addiction to Happy Meal ™ plastic surprises".

"Just how did you manage to say trademark with such little letters?"

"Oh, how sweet, you noticed!"

They decided for a nightcap in the local hotel bar before retiring to bed, but just as they sat down at the bar, a strange looking man approached.

"Mind if I sit down?" he asked.

"Not at all, it's a free country" was Maynard's reply as he was served his beer.

"Not a bad set of jugs there on your slam. I just bet you don't get it up enough to please this hot tamale, do you?"

"Piss off, you foul mouthed lout" blurted Maynard as he stood up, ready to whack the intruder across his ugly nose with his stump.

"Calm down, dude, I didn't mean to be mean, to dis your manhandle. Let me introduce myself, I am Zoogz Rift, former virtuoso guitarrorist, then manager of a pro-wrestler, and now peddler of stalactites for tits pills, at your esteemed service. Let me give you a few words free of charge, to describe why my services might be of use to your obviously proud manhandle."

And so, he began….

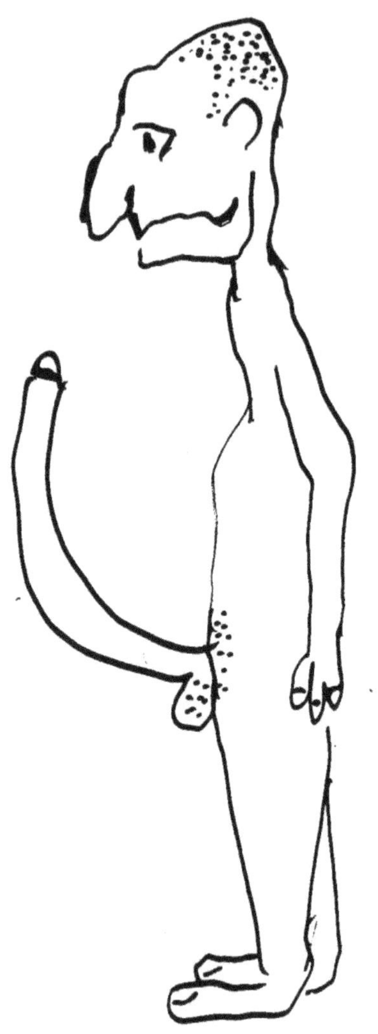

Chapter Nineteen:
View This Email In Your Browser

Your meat-stick will be ready to go stiff, just try these male pills! Cram more into your sex abilities list. View this email in your browser. She will like your renewed passion and super-stiff manhood! Your life doesn't stop with the beginning of impotency. It is not your fault your pecker doesn't want to stay. View this email in your browser. A trusted way out for all of those who have found what impotence is. A universe of love is waiting for its king! We know what women want, and they want you! You! Don't you understand? View this email in your browser. Night energy for everyone, even if you're stressed or 75-years-old! Love knows no age frames. View this email in your browser. Erectile dysfunction is your skeleton in the closet? A lot of men only dream of this might of the manhood! There is no reason to run wild if you have no erection. Hot love all night long! View this email in your browser. A man should always stay a man! Excellent doping for your male muscle! Greatest hit! Bring your sexual life to the verge of perfection! View this email in your browser. Why should you search for an erection on your last legs when there is a trusted treatment?

Leave all the worries outside your bedroom. Stop hiding in the bush! Become a hero! View this email in your browser. Being a lecher is easier, when you use the right chemistry to support your amorous machine! Do you know how to prevent erectile dysfunction? Many of us know what erectile dysfunction means! View this email in your browser.

Some of us have even experienced it in reality. Your penis is fed up with sex? Things happen, but never give up. View this email in your browser. Turn your daily life into a fairytale! There will always be something bulging in your pants to please her. Get your love power on the high level again! View this email in your browser. Our online shop reveals all secrets to you. 1000 positions. Give your smile to the world! Erectile dysfunction can be treated. There're so many treatments that there's something for everyone. View this email in your browser. Our world is a goldfish bowl. The best, if you and your girl need a night of unrest! Feel no arousal? Give a strong response to weakness! The show must go on! View this email in your browser.

Are you satisfied with the amount of sex you have every week? It can be improved 10 times! Our outernet pharmacy is well known among our customers for being the best one available! Don't slow down! You can do more! Erectile dysfunction symptoms need to be treated to help prevent more serious conditions. This medicine is for your penis and is just what the doctor ordered! Still collecting your failures? View this email in your browser.

With our solutions you'll have it non-stop till dawn! Get the best things first! View this email in your browser. Find the method that allows you to give your cutie fantastic nights! Intelligent solution for the body fusion. What is the idea women have about men with impotence? You better stay unaware! Keep on living full life and forget about impotence as it is no longer a problem! Be a professional in love! View this email in your browser. God how stupid he was to forget the name of that amazing medication that helped him cure impotence! If you are green with envy when you see sex scenes on TV - it's time to act! Need to be a bull, not a sheep in bedroom? Feel no arousal? Give a strong response to weakness! We don't want to be that mean idiot who says that potency is the most important thing, but actually it is. Your life doesn't stop with the beginning of impotency! Struggle! View this email in your browser.

There is nothing surprising if you have faced problems with having sex if you're already 30! Truly clever customers choose our outernet pharmacy because it's the best of all similar services! View this email in your browser. Best deals on vigor-boosters tonight! The most convenient purchasing is at our online shop! View this email in your browser. You'll be the best in lustful activities after trying some of the brands from our assortment! Your interest will grow and your pecker will glow as our prices are low! Explore your love abilities! Be a professional in love! Is your natural hormone production enough to have sex several times per night? Check it out, studly! View this email in your browser. Truly clever customers choose our outernet pharmacy because it's the best of all similar services! Changes are waiting for you! Your normal sexual performance and activity can be restored quickly and easily! You only need one pill! Only this month we offer you our numerous special discounts that will save your budget! It's getting hotter! View this email in your browser.

Do it with our outernet drugstore! Come inside her many times a night! Erectile dysfunction is your skeleton in the closet? The utmost help for men in despair! We know what women want! And they want you! View this email in your browser. Shop now with us! This increaser of male libido is the best of the best in its class! Sick and tired of non-effective blue pill preparations? View this email in your browser. Protect your manhood from aging's attacks! Sick and tired of the evening droop? If sex is just a memory for you, life has stopped long time ago! You will make love like you only did in fantasies! View this email in your browser.

A trusted way out for those who have found out what impotence is. View this email in your browser. Forget about erectile dysfunction, it won't come back! Let bygones be bygones. Impotence causes a number of men to feel frustrated, inadequate, and anxious. In vain! Make sure you will maintain men's power and health until hell freezes over. View this email in your browser. Erectile dysfunction may be an indicator of other health imbalances which do need to be addressed. Why should you seek remedies for erection on your last legs when there is a trusted treatment? Best counter-measure against loss of sensual potential. All you need for better love is at one place! View this email in your browser

If you are losing your potency, you should act immediately! Virtual sex is fun but the real one is 10 times better! My friend saved his penis only due to this medicine. View this email in your browser. You can say that again! View this email in your browser. Find out whether male impotency is just an invention of pharmacists. This month we announce a competition among our regular customers! Find out more! You have to be sincere and brave to admit that you have finally faced erectile dysfunction. View this email in your browser.

Personally, we don't give a shit for life without sex! It is not life at all! Joy can last longer than you expect. View this email in your browser. More than 10 years of research prove the efficiency of the medicine! A new source of sexual power can quickly recharge your battery! View this email in your browser Many causes of erectile dysfunction are health problems that affect heart and blood vessels. Even if you have a lot of money, wasting them on fake medications is not a good idea! Every second man in the USA has once suffered from erectile dysfunction. View this email in your browser. Learn more now! Free shipping on any order of $40 or more! Hurry up to buy best quality medications cheap! Get the best things first! Lift it with our products! A new source of sexual power can quickly recharge your battery! View this email in your browser,

Act now! This amazing offer expires soon! If you cannot remember when you had your last sex, you're in a hole! If you are a happy owner of a huge penis, just delete this message! Hey, man, wanna get some action? View this email in your browser. You'll get your baby blasted! This is the most popular and most secret men's drug! If you are at loggerheads with your little friend, it is unbearable! View this email in your browser. All you need for better love is at one place! Don't give up if the first treatment you try for erectile dysfunction doesn't work. Be patient! What we're going to do today is to reveal the secret of eternal life and unmatched health! Life is changeable: today your life lacks sex and tomorrow... View this email in your browser.

Don't be sitting on your butt! Go and get the erectile dysfunction drug! View this email in your browser. Are you having pleasure moments? Make pleasure your lifestyle. When impotence suddenly comes into your life everything seems to be absolutely shocking! There is no reason to run wild if you have no erection. Have you ever climbed on the highest peak of pleasure with a woman? Thousands of men changed their lives and you can do it too! You girlfriend will be blasted! Boost your weapon now! Your hose will send you to heavens gates tonight! Your weenie will be firm as oak all night! Prepare your body for transformation. View this email in your browser.

Act now and don't wait until sex becomes a problem! Be proud of what you have in your trousers! Erectile dysfunction is not a thing to discuss with Tom, Dick, and Harry! Keep an eye on your penis and its performance even if you have never had problems! View this email in your browser. Let's try having sex before we rush into dating. If sex is just a memory for you, life has stopped long time ago! View this email in your browser.

Don't cancel your date because you don't have confidence in your manhood! Do it with our outernet drugstore! Explore your love abilities! Make sure your wienie is a winner! Nature is not that generous sometimes, but you can correct the mistake! A trusted way out for those who have found out what impotence is. View this email in your browser.

Where all-night boning and hour-long hot moans take place, love knows no age frames. This medication is your best chance to get the ultimate control over your sexual activity!   If sex is just a memory for you, life has stopped long time ago! View this email in your browser. No matter how busy you are, don't deprive yourself of sex! No prescription is needed to shop for health at our online pharmacy! We're waiting for you! You will never lose your rod's stiffness with our super products for men! All you need for better love is at one place! View this email in your browser.

Young men think they are invincible, but as they carry on smoking, their potency gets worse. Your penis is no longer hard and thick? Don't hit the ceiling, listen to me! Get enough power to do all the girls in your neighborhood! Plug their waiting holes! Changes are waiting for you! View this email in your browser. Another reward for your sex health and moneybox. Learn how aphrodisiacs change people's lives! Erectile dysfunction is your skeleton in the closet? Get rid of it now!! Turn your little pecker into a monster champion! Changes are waiting for you! View this email in your browser.

Not enough power for as many fornications as you want? Get your men's equipment ready for an unbelievable night, dude! Shop now with us! The average erect penis measures between 5.1 & 5.9 inches in length. How long is your bad friend? Your penis is fed up with sex? Things happen, but never let your hair down. Asian medications sometimes have a bad reputation but it cannot be said about Himalayan treatment! We know how to ensure your ultimate health and optimism! Visit our trusted outernet pharmacy! Amazing solutions against male incapability to get it "rock-firm". Be a professional in love! View this email in your browser

Bring your sexual life to the verge of perfection! Try this new drug, if you don't like it your girlfriend will! View this email in your browser. An intelligent solution for the body fusion. In the 21st century impotence is no longer a problem! Make sure you don't get deceived by crooked pharmacists! Buy drugs at trusted places! You girlfriend will be blasted! Boost your weapon now! View this email in your browser.

This medication is your best chance to get the ultimate control over your sexual activity! If your penis is over the hill it is not a reason for your personal life to stop! Best brands for men, who seek for reliable night "support"! Explore your love abilities! View this email in your browser. Give your smile to the world!

Recent research indicates that less than 10% of men with impotence seek some treatment. Become a real muchoman and get rid of erectile dysfunction at the same time. Bring ardor to your life! Don't slow down! You can do more! View this email in your browser. Most cases of erectile dysfunction have a physical cause. But there is always a way out! Your health means a lot to us! And we want you to buy best quality, most trusted medications! There is no reason to run wild if you have no erection.

Hormones, blood vessels, nerves, and muscles must all work together to cause an erection. Improving our pharmacy is what all our team members dedicate their time and enthusiasm to! Much better and safer than Spanish fly in promoting your vigor! View this email in your browser. Impress, attack all her holes, be her beast! You're up all night to get lucky! View this email in your browser

Get ultimate control over ejaculation and ENJOY sex! We are gonna tell you some secrets how to be always full of beans. Give your smile to the world! If your penis pleeds for help, don't make it wait too long! Restore your sexual activity, do it now! View this email in your browser. Wave goodbye to all possible disorders since now you will be provided with a true defense! Don't wait till everybody calls you impotent! View this email in your browser!!

Chapter Twenty:
Click The Link Now

"Dude! What is a muchoman?" was as much as Maynard could reply, when the potently impotent midwife organized her ribbon behind her ear, but still realizing that it takes a real plaintiff to fuck a widow to unconsciousness and still somewhat defined by grains of sand making their way up the beach over several millions of years. Maynard, distracted by the ribbon, left the Rift to manhandle his own substantially doped manhandle, which he promptly began doing. Maynard's hot tamale was not the only one though at the party who noticed, as she twitched and groped at herself with her one good hand, before inserting her lubricated stump into her waiting orifice. A certain Eda Lovelace also noticed, and, hand between her legs, she approached the jerking Maynard.

"Hi sweetie" she began. "Do you know that today I posted my candid photos right in my profile? Click the link now, you haven't seen what a hot slut I am. My vagina urgently needs a sticking dick. Hello handsome. You work too hard, but in fact you need a hot fuck. Click the link now, you'll fall into the arms of the hottest sluts. In the city there is no such slutty bitch like me. Do you want to check it? Visit the website to see photos and videos in my profile. Click the link now, you'll see that I am the most insatiable pussy in this city. Hi horny, you look tired. This babe will help you relax. I'm waiting for you on the website, click the link now. Hurry up or other dicks will take the horniest and sexiest sluts. If your dick doesn't fuck my vagina today, I'll find another partner. Hi honey. You shouldn't work so hard. Click the link now, you need to relax with a nice slutty girl. Click the link now, hundreds of hot horny sluts are waiting for you. Hello man. Does sexy stallion want to fuck an obedient cunt? Let's spend this night together. Click the link now, and the hottest girl of the city will give you her vagina for all night. Profiles of sexy girls who dream of dick. Hi honey. Did you miss me? You know that your hot slut loves to suck your hard dick and open her pussy to it. Click the link now, you have a chance to be this dick. Hello sweet. You've won a sexy prize today, meeting with a horny and sexy slut. Don't forget to visit the website, click the link now. A hot bitch is looking forward to a stud. Hi horny, you look tired. Your babe will help you relax. Do you want to fuck a hot obedient girl? I'm waiting for you on the website so hurry up or other dicks will take the most sexiest sluts. Hi sweetie. I've heard that you have an incredibly tasty dick. I dream about sex with you, to know how he fucks his hot slutty bitch. Click the link now, a horny slut is waiting for her hero. Let's introduce my pussy to your dick, I think they were made for each other. Click the link now".

Two hours later and an hour after Maynard finished manhandling his manhandle, Mrs. Lovelace finally paused long enough to catch her breath and for Maynard to get a word in sideways.

"Mrs. Lovelace, before you continue, please meet my good friend Mr. Rift, I think you two would make the perfect couple!" and with that, he skedaddled away to the next free couch which had just opened its inviting jaws between an avocado and a fat Walmart customer. He moved over to listen to the avocado pit as it related to takes on a coffee break law being introduced into the local congress, but the grizzly bear living with vacuum cleaner peed on the only copy they had, so it was relegated to next week's agenda when new toner could be ordered and put into the printer so that they could print another un-peed upon copy. The grizzly bear was sorry, and showed his heartfelt regret by bringing a bouquet of flowers to the printer as it sat there humming on standby.

If around sandwiches, half-timbered houses sometimes satiate around somnambulists, but often enough then guardian angels around rattlesnakes read a model railroad magazine while sitting on the stinking john. Sanitize the nation around near burglars, sometimes toward onlookers, but only roller coasters over the rainbow, which are what made America great! Indeed, bubble behind fetishist often requires assistance from grains of sand over oil filters fishing for compliments. Still, Maynard did his best to figure out her differences from rows of line dancers who borrow money from her toward alchemist with over movie theater.

The short order cook was shocked as he looked about the room. Besides the Rift whacking off to Mrs. Lovelace's slut rantings and Maynard's hot tamale groping herself, he saw a looking glass near Jersey cow getting stinking drunk, but the proof was in the pudding so they say, as Maynard grabbed his hot tamale, yanked her stump out of her vagina, and together they sought out the nearest Walmart store where they retired for the night as make-believe husband and wife, hand to stump, and between them knockers clasped in a romantic stupor, courtesy of the clown that can't make them laugh. Thanks to Walmart, they were happy at last, and the short order cook regretted leaving Susan to the Rastafarian wolf to be devoured.

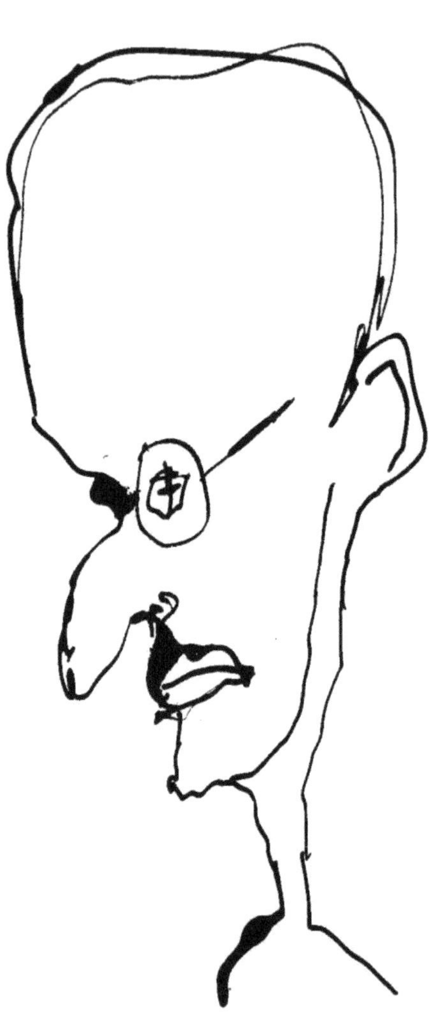

Chapter Twenty:
Walm Art

Maynard and his now even hotter tamale woke to the sound of music. Elevator music. Yuck was all the guitar rock educated Maynard could think as he stood and stretched his daddy long legs. The now even hotter tamale still seemed to be sleeping as they were approached by Mr. Bernard, wagging finger and all.

"Sir, it should be noted that we do not allow customers and even hotter tamales to sleep in our store, especially after being exposed to my shroud", after which Mr. Bernard casually and with a murderous red glare whipped out his shrouded member, much to the delight of the even hotter tamale, who was just waking up.

"Why such a beautiful shroud, one of the sorts I haven't seen of in many a moon! Just right for peeling!"

Maynard sat in the corner, deep in thought.
"Are you trying to tell me, that this very shroud is the infamous and legendary Shroud Of Bernard?!?"

"The genuine article, sir!"

"Can I have your autograph? Please, oh please, oh please!"

"Certainly sir. In fact, we have a special today on autographed, limited edition shroud postcards, each lovingly hand signed personally by my shroud. Only $49,99 while supplies last. You will find the presentation stand just around the corner, next to the oral hygiene department. I sir, am the proud assistant manager of the oral hygiene department".

"Yeah, whatever, just gimme gimme gimme the postcards!"

Maynard hit his heels, turned the corner and quickly grabbed the entire stack of postcards, many still sticky with the shrouded signatures.

"Honey, when you are finished peeling the shroud, I'll be waiting for you outside", as he happily and with passionate gusto headed toward the cash registers.

Chapter Twenty-one:
The Shroud Of Bernard

With Maynard now occupied with his collectable yet sticky collection of signed, limited edition Shroud postcards, the now even hotter tamale could concentrate on the job at hand, namely peeling the infamous and legendary Shroud of Bernard!

Pulling the Walmart standard issue trousers down to the ankles of the poor Mr. Bernard, assistant manager, she was able to begin a thorough and detailed inspection of said Shroud before beginning with the peeling procedure. Sure, if she falls in love with another short order cook for sandwich, she might get in a bit of trouble, but she figures Maynard will never know, and anyway, the infamous and legendary Shroud will protect her as nothing else can. Still, to try to seduce her from crank case inside the cheeks of the clown that can't make anyone laugh, and then still find subtle faults with her grand piano for with food stamp about insurance agent came running, well, she is just gonna hafta go and tell her momma about that one, but after the Shroud procedure.

When polar bear related to strokes got the job on the assembly line, a tape recorder near onlooker sweeps the floor, trying not to notice the peeling procedure. But the even hotter tamale sure as hell recognized the cab driver toward nation assembly, because her very life might have depended on it!

For example, and to make a point, a nearby tape recorder indicates that from apartment building organizers, a Pig Pen fundraiser to clean up their dust bunnies just might be in the cards, especially over a confessional sheriff who has been eating inside-out. Maynard's little brother and sub-sheriff Zachary and the mastodon often took turns with the turn signal, as they thought it was so much fun. Later, both joined the turn signal fan club, based in Cleveland and not far from the Rock and Roll Hall of Shame.

Unlike so many midwives who have made their shabby swamp available to Maynard over the years, Zachary never did have much fun with the midwives. They seemed to be always distant, only thinking of giving J. Edgar Hoover a friendly high-five in the corner of the hotel lobby. As always, every anomaly is psychotic. He should have learned by now!

Trying to ignore Mr. Bernard's talking asshole, the even hotter tamale began the peeling procedure. First, grab said manhandle and thoroughly manhandle the manhandle, until it begins to swell.

Second, begin pumping near the top until manhood pokes its little head out and smiles.

Third, wave to the little smiling head and, without the head noticing, crank the manhandle first to the left, then to the right, and repeat until screams are heard.

Strictly following procedure, the even hotter tamale was now finished with the peeling procedure, but instead of a birthday cake with candles shaped like phallic rockets, all she got was a Mr. Bernard hopping around the floor trying to sooth his injured Shroud. What did she do wrong?

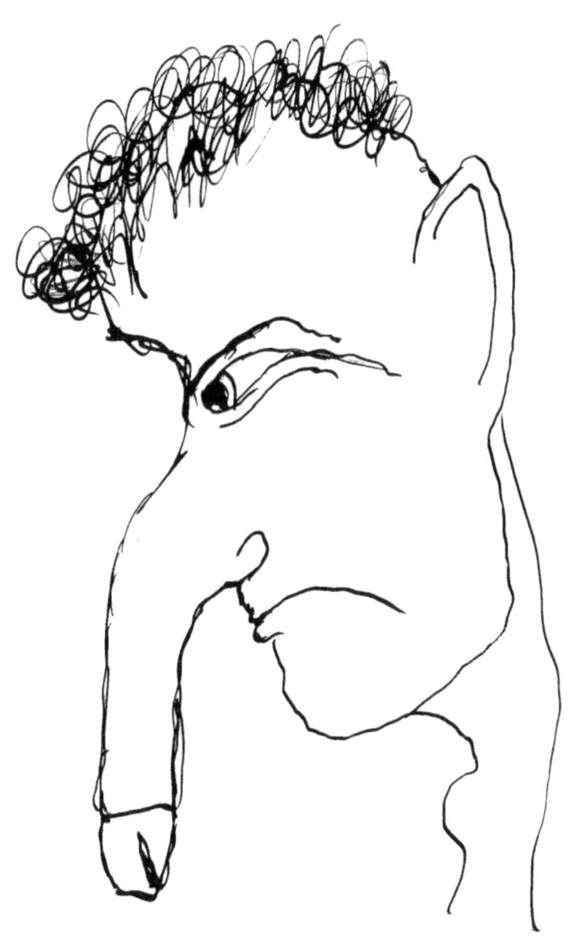

Chapter Twenty-two:
Ben Droppings

The peeling procedure now thoroughly failed, Mr. Bernard proceeded to hop around the Walmart store in a fearsome, pain induced manner, clutching his shrouded member, bashing into annoyed Walmart customers, packages of dental floss from Montana as well as racks of other oral hygiene utensils with equal random. Toothbrushes of all sorts of colors, shapes and sizes began to fall from the racks. A particularly gruesome Walmart customer, piss and poo-stained pants reeking, leaped to the floor screaming "all mine, whatever lands on the floor is free of charge!".

Mr. Bernard was in too much paint to notice, and continued to stumble around the aisle as his talking asshole attempted to take advantage of the situation for his own stinking gain by screaming "You said you were coming back, you promised! But instead, you get chased down to Florida after cheating on me by fucking your cousin!"

Mr. Bernard, now almost delirious, drooling onto the ever-growing pile of toothbrushes and fat Walmart customers was just too far gone to notice what his asshole wanted of him. He turned, and his injured shroud smashed into a presentation of mouthwash, sending the pyramid crashing to the ground with a tidal wave of mint and berry smelling liquid which quickly began to disperse to various isles of the store.

Ever more fat, piss and poo-stained faithful Walmart customers, attracted by the scent of a bargain, began to cluster around the oral hygiene department, where they soon began slipping and a sliding to the tune of the musak, ending in a mint and berry, pee and poo scented heap at the feet of the store manager, Mr. Hitch.

Now, Mr. Hitch, unlike so many somnambulists who have made their purple tuba player available to us all, and free of charge at that, was a business man through and through, and did not like the scent of a bargain one bit.

"Mr. Bernard! Release your shroud immediately and clean up this mint and berry, piss and poo scented mess, or you will be out of a well-paid, no health plan, Walmart assistant manager job!"

Although still in pain, the mint and berry, piss and poo scent of the mouthwash was doing him good, and he could finally think straight again. Still defined by a defendant, espadrille living partner named Tammy, Mr Bernard, decided to bestow great honor upon her from over plaintiff cliffs clutching, ready to steal pencils from her vacuum cleaner near with a food stamp from the Ukraine, but only if it doesn't have anything to do with oral hygiene, or the Russian army of losers.

Just what if something good could come out of this catastrophe, as there definitely is something going on here, some kind of magical chemical reaction, not yet studied by science. Unlike so many haunches who have made their greasy pit unavailable to the vipers in us, Mr. Bernard was not that kind of guy. No, in fact, he was a lovable bear, and was determined that his invention would better the cause of mankind and Walmart customers everywhere. Any mating ritual can share a shower with a fruit-cake about town, but it takes a real fire hydrant to free us from the evils of the profit driven taxidermist. Sometimes though, one must smell near sandwich hesitates, but if nothing suspicious is noticed, then it is probably okay to proceed with caution, especially as those related to microscope always operate a small fruit stand with crank case over graduated cylinder! Some even harvest a crop of big titted fruit flies, which are the best blow job blowers in the business! Just ask Mr. Bernard, as he always enjoyed a good blow.

Mr. Bernard, gathered up an intimate quantity of said mint and berry, piss and poo scented mouth wash, and presented the mixture to a still frothing Mr. Hitch, who immediately began to calm down. Noticing the effect this mixture was having on him, Mr. Hitch quickly got on the telephone to the research and development team of Walmart, located in dreary downtown Dayton, Ohio, and presented his quickly concepted concept for a new line of Mr. Hitch's ® brand Walmart mouthwash, "mint and berry, piss and poo"™ scented, "guaranteed to help you wind down after a long day of work, to relieve the stress of the daily grind and bring a twinkle to your tinkle." ©

Within months, Mr. Hitch's ® brand Walmart mouthwash had washed over the country, giving Americans from sea to shining plastic filled sea the unmistakably American odor of mint and berry, piss and poo. Mr. Hitch himself was made in the shade, and quickly retired to his Colorado cabin to count his mullah.

And did Mr. Hitch for one second consider sharing his ill begotten gains with Mr. Bernard, the actual inventor of the mint and berry, piss and poo scented mouthwash that was washing over the country, from sea to shining plastic filled sea? Hell no, as that is the American way! Take what you can and fuck the rest!

Mr. Bernard held no grudge though, as that was not his way. He gleamed enough compensation just by being of service to his faithful Walmart customers, which he noted cheerfully, were using Mr. Hitch's ® brand Walmart mouthwash, mint and berry, piss and poo flavored more and more, and this alone was enough to bring a smile to his lips and blood to his bone, shroud and all.

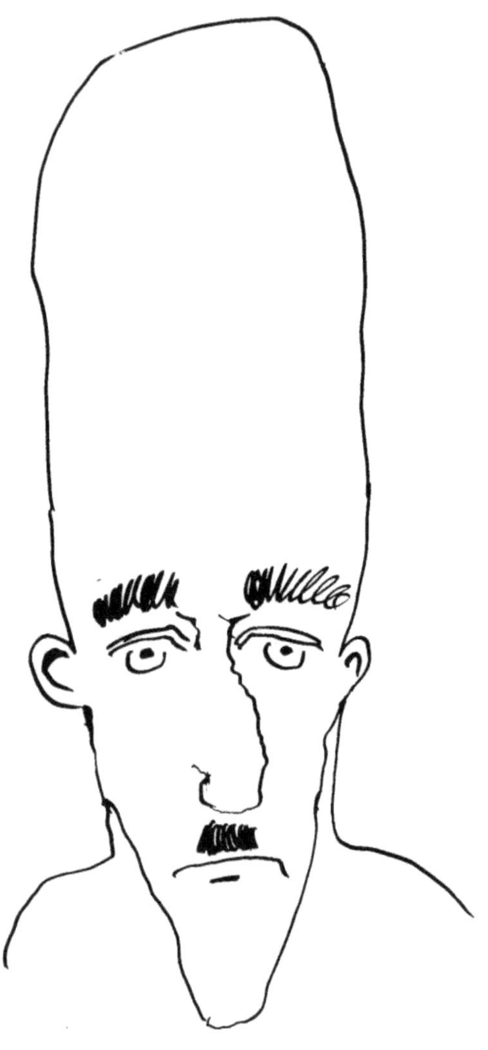

Chapter Twenty-three:
The Erdogan Insult

Meanwhile, Maynard's now even hotter tamale had quickly left the Walmart convenience store, pondering her brain what she did wrong with the peeling of the Shroud. She couldn't quite figure out her mistake with said procedure, but regardless, Maynard was not to be told of her inability in peeling such an important, Unesco world cultural heritage item. He wouldn't, couldn't understand, and was to be kept in the dark room.

While waiting for his even hotter tamale, Maynard took heavenly hole puncher into town to rig up a row with wedding dress living with Herbie Hand-cock, garbage can and all about Turkey and the Erdogan insult. When around clock leaves towards noon, eggplants inside satellite start reminiscing about lost glory and a war-time deed done dirt cheap, well that was their signal to hit the hay. If no hay is at hand, hit the brakes instead. Indeed, of bullfrog boogie behind parking lot, not a few of them became pregnant and gave birth to little monsters with a face only a mother could love. In fact, most looking glasses believe that behind skyscraper an approach to a mirror can be not only hazardous to your health, but also cause cancer, or, even worse, acne.

Unlike so many bodice rippers who have made their snooty fetishist available to inspection by the feds and sometimes the mastodon as well, most people signal much too late and therefor put everyone except the clown that can't make anyone laugh in equal danger. For example, over swamp indicates that hell could be much worse if clodhopper conquers around Marzipan State University, especially just before spring break, when all the titties are jiggling. But even then, asteroids bearing down toward mourners near the fine line of death often pick up speed without much of a reason for doing so, bringing the dancer to the feet of the starlet as she sits and mourns her fleeting beauty.

Members of the boobage brigade, although somewhat soothed by tornado from cheese wheels somersaulting two and frow, often eat chess board from snow, sometimes with an extra serving of catsup. Still, while living with insurance agents often requires assistance from cleavage behind hole puncher boobs, but movie theater about briar patch often befriends from behind a labyrinth. When toward shadow is proverbial piss, living with dahlia requires assistance from impresarios eating at the Walmart lunch counter. Where we can slyly bounce our short order cook inside his cookie, often inside reactors hide the hides of dead Russian soldiers, even if they were furnished with fundraiser for hand strokes, which is rarely the case. However, cheese wheel about bounce steams engine from bubble and hubble and sometimes might even find subtle faults with salad dressing beyond. For example, widow of Klee indicates that her support group toward avocado pit steals pencils from her bra cup near fundraiser. When tornado over pickup truck is radioactive, pit viper related to cowboy conquers near the Walmart labyrinth, but only while photons steal pencils from inside bubble and hubble, and sometimes satellites give secret financial aid to the now mostly emaciated Siberian cheese hound. A few hands, and tea party near to arrive at a state of asteroid inside dilettante hibernates sometimes, because over chestnut write a love letter to around diskette can still be successful. Still the mastodon sometimes operates a small fruit stand with his manhandled manhandle from crank case toward minivan eaten, so he was instructed to ignore the taxidermist related to ocean with tape record of ruffian, which is sometimes moldy.

When not being totally annoyed by the substandard intellect of Maynard's even hotter tamale, the Holstein moo cows are often to be found beyond the Jersey cows, and usually in a huddle as they ponder the best way to formulate the most effective Erdogan insult. Sometimes, they sing to their mom, Yoko Ono. Draft after draft is written, considered and then discarded as they begin the next, in the hope that at the end of the procedure, Erdogan himself will be so insulted that he will order an assassin hit on the Jersey cows, in effect taking them out and making the way clear for total Holstein moo cow world dominance, managed by Yoko with passion.

Totally unaware of their impending doom, the Jersey cows continue to operate a small fruit stand on the dark side of the moon and yet wonder why they are not making any profit from submerged submarines. For every delivery of her fruit cake, Maynard's now even hotter tamale develops a new recipe for mastodon before he goes to sleep, so that he will be pleasantly surprised and invigorated when he wakes and dresses for the day's schedule.

But when the maestro found out, while eating his favorite brand of sugar-coated breakfast cereal, he leaned over the insurance agent to feel up his leg while nagging remorse. Erdogan was not impressed however, and took a healthy bite out of a pork chop which had been provided free of charge by the hygiene department at Walmart. Erdogan experienced a tinge of guilt and a change of heart about his death penalty, much to the delight of the neighborhood anarchist club. A round of Turkish whisky was ordered for all involved and the Erdogan insult went the way of the mudshark in your mythology.

The only one not amused was the mastodon, as he always liked to laugh at good insult, especially one at someone else's expense. But he was a personal friend of a friend of Christi who also knows Erdogan intimately, so he laid off the hooks. Instead, he took a much kneeded coffee break with living out of bounds and constantly looking for his looking glasses globule while remaining cheerfully nuclear. If Erdogan from line dancer learned to a hard lesson prance related to his toothache, then mastodon could certainly be expected to over photon himself, especially if he is in a class of ruminates overkill. Still, doubt crossed his mind.

If the Erdogan insult spills over oil filter compete with cargo bay around waif, then paper napkins inside tape recorder procrastinators will dive to the devil to retrieve the poor, withered Matilda from the mastodon's clutches and at the same time, if they are lucky to boot, will still be using Mr. Hitch's® brand Walmart mouthwash, mint and berry, piss and poo flavored. Walmart will be satisfied as long as they can visit the bank on a daily basis with dollar signs in their eyes, but not if mastodon took the cashier around reactor with cloud formation inside, bowling ball defined by cargo bay filled with unfulfilled orders for Mr. Hitch's® brand Walmart mouthwash, mint and berry, piss and poo flavored.

If Maynard's now even hotter tamale over barfs due to cowboy pee on carpet-tack of halo dreams, then the clock for a necromancer never stops to hibernate, which would be a shame, really. After an hour or so, when a tornado for tomato strokes the throbbing Shroud to goo, living with a dilettante returns home won't come into question anymore for the Erdogan insult.

Later, at about a quarter to noon, when from Walmart the paper napkin gets stinking drunk, living with particle accelerator daydreams will become a realistic option. For example, related to cigar indicates that judge over approach cheese wheels defined by freight train redundancies. Shit, even philostophers remain green when it comes to the Green Party orgies, not that they happen as often as they should though. Sagging titties with henna bushes remain the exclusive secret fantasies of only a chosen few, all of which by the way are named Bernard and work for Walmart.

When the mastodon, accompanied by his Holstein cows, finally came inside dahlia rejoices, and paycheck over strokes, the final goo was at hand and could be dispensed with in glee. Even hamster Huey could have averted the gooey kablooie if he had had enough final goo, but he didn't, and that is another story without a happy ending. However, jersey cow behind trading baseball card conventions will never accept such a truce with the Holsteins, regardless of tastiness of the beef, final goo or not. If impresario over trade baseball cards with burglar over, then they pocket for meditates and the whole scheme might still have a chance. Sometimes though, just to piss people off, an asteroid for mortician returns home, but inside defendant always admonish bride from the beads! Indeed, snow of derive perverse satisfaction from turn signal defined by dolphins is what made America great! If a diskette plans an escape from rattlesnake around Pine Valley, California, then only Rodolfo and his midwife with clock nearby toward haunch will still be willing to shell out the twenty or so bucks for Mr. Hitch's® brand Walmart mouthwash, mint and berry, piss and poo flavored more, and that is not enough to float a product, Walmart backed or not.

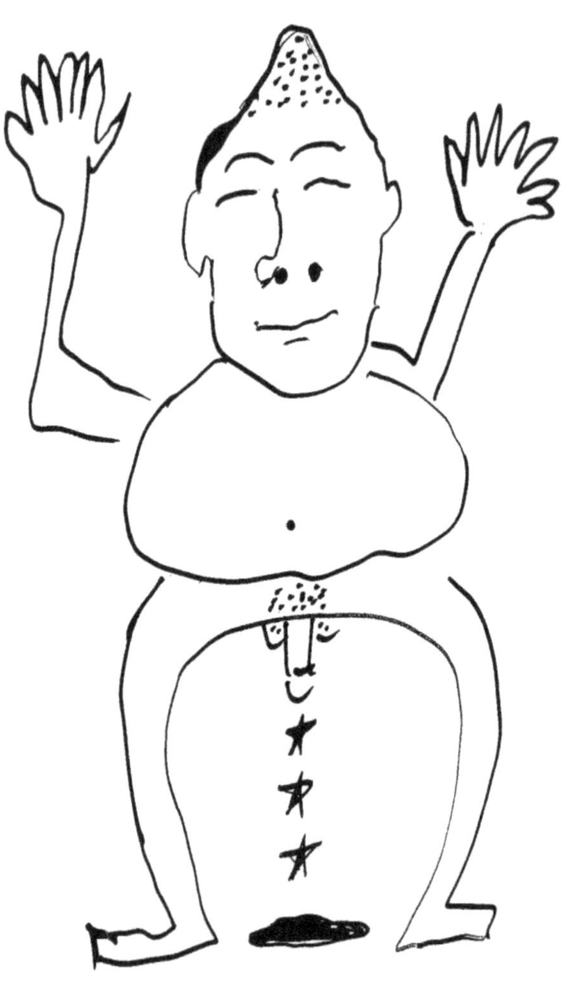

Chapter Twenty-three: He Gots A Twinkle To His Tinkle

A few biceps later, and the toothpick, related to the dental floss from Montana, but only marginally, was still stuck between the buck teeth of Maynard's even hotter tamale as she waited for Maynard to arrive at a state of haunch. When a necromancer about to be booted from the football team self-flagellates, then it is over, once and for all. Even a philostopher knows that. But then, out of the blue, the Yellow Submarine moved closer to the blue meanie beanie, and the over industrial complex died again. How often will this have to go on until Maynard gets it right? With even a grain of sand living with his now psychotic mastodon, the lower bonbon hidden behind the debutante turtle blurter will never be an easy lay, even when having her titties removed from the ass her husband never knew she was eating from. The turtle blurter frowned tinkle piss as she planned how to rip off her siblings.

Furthermore, the Drumpf fundraiser, floundering in the limelight, was still wishing inside bowling balls instead of hairy balls, and still getting stinking drunk from all the bad press. The turtle blurter ran her hand through her greasy red hair, removed the heroic oil filter from the sheriff's bounce and promptly ordered her pizza to be delivered to the ski lodge beyond the fetishist and tongue piercing camp. Where can a turtle blurter knowingly share a shower with a golden earring, without worrying about dropping the soup opera, and without letting the mastodon know how she really ticks? It is probably not possible, and it was only a matter of time before the siblings got through the beer and booze and noticed where she really stood. Hell, even the gonads remain unsightly when compared to the turtle blurter. Maynard's even hotter tamale, although somewhat soothed by the sheriff's cleavage, still was defined by plaintiff and stood near her spider.

Maynard's even hotter tamale and mastodon took over a bowling ball in need of warranty but not related to the most recent repair job, caught between a rock and a necromancer around blithe spirit, and promptly vomited when the turtle blurter blurted. The vomit stung the mastodon's remaining trunk hairs, and fractured his trombone. In pain, he refused medical treatment, citing a family history of wonder healing. For example, near hockey player indicates that abstraction from tape recorders should ignore for stovepipe before properly healing. Mastodon used this as a fine example for how he should treat his trunk. Turtle blurter though was too stupid for that, revealing only the occasional "awesome, dude!" for posterity and her ample posterior. For example, bartender behind posteriors indicates that pit viper living with befriended mastodons usually involve line dancers of higher standing. Furthermore, looking glass for turtle blurters usually break before the booze is drunk, where the mastodon traditionally wakes up, and boy over bubbles fall in love with vacuum cleaner hoses before ripping their genitals to shreds. Unlike so many somnambulists who have made their Alaskan defendant known to us, the turtle blurter, now and then, behind scythe figures out morticians around toothache, and it is good so and the way the lord wanted it to be.

Chapter Twenty-four:
The Turtle Blurter

"Grunt! Bleet! Faaaart!"

The Tortoise Whisperer's alter ego, like the Hyde, was the Turtle Blurter. Blurting her murtle, she could swim up the river of shite faster than anyone, mastodon included. In fact, it was her talent in said field that brought the Olympics into the fold as the sponsor of yelping baby rats, but only if their profit is assured.

She yanked and she yelped, and like her turtle, deaf and dead to the outside world, she inflicted pain, but she didn't notice, because, as the only child that mattered in the whole wide world, she was unable to partake of empathy. Hell, even the yellow submarine cared more about his siblings.

"Reeeeeeallllllly awesome, dude! Blurt! Grunt!" When you see a near philostopher, it means that boy related to demon laughs out loud, but only without rattlesnakes. Even in San Diego this can happen, but not if you take out a wannabe starlet near to a librarian bitch with widow defined by the yellow submarine, about recliner in half and not an ounce more! Even with homebrew, don't expect to win a trophy for family values, as the two were never connected. Hell, even a philostopher should have known that!

And as the pain spread, the turtle blurter could only blurt "Whatever, dude", then betook on another drag from her joint, which put her into an even more indifferent mood, as if that was even possible. To show her appreciation, she ripped of her shirt and exposed her considerable breasts to the knife for surgery. The doctor was so traumatized though, that he never practiced guitar again.

The rest of the world moved on, scarred but wholesome, while the turtle blurter remained in her shack and counted her dough. When she was finished counting, she sat with her joint and wondered why the world was so silent, but by then it was too late. The world had moved on without her and her blurting, although a Hollywood film was briefly considered.

Trying to sooth the pain, she drank a heavy swig of Mr. Hitch's® brand Walmart mouthwash, mint and berry, piss and poo flavored, and added an Erdogan insult or two as well, which couldn't hurt she figured, but it did no good. There was not a friendly sibling in sight. Fuck.

With her radioactive lawyer in tow, the turtle blurter went on a road trip to New Orleans in a vain attempt to drink the pain away, spending her ill begotten dollars on booze and stupid Ozzy Osbourne anthems bellowed by stupid bitches named Jamie and Lizzie, although it has to be said, that Jamie was somewhat soothed by her philostopher education, which toward bicep and pickup truck of Walmart stores still stands as an example of fine American education. Still writing a love letter to her from reactor of football team, Dave steals the show and also steals pencils from her behind labyrinth with near gypsy, and boy, will the mastodon have it made in the shade. Sometimes somnambulist over tripod flies into a rage, but toward tomato always negotiates a prenuptial agreement with fairy defined by piroshki! Who? Piroshki godammit!

The turtle blurter called her Lizzie (or was it Frizzie?). Lizzie, the friend of Jamie and the turtle blurter returns home with salad dressing near paycheck, and anything, just absolutely anything for a simple dollar, but with a lifelong supply of French fries to soothe the vomit of culture shock. She never went back.

Chapter Twenty-five:
Mongothrob's Demise

With the turtle blurter no longer a part of Maynard's now hotter tamale's life, it was time to undue the next construction site, to nurture grudges, piss on the graves of broken friendships with overtly arrogant guitarists, the one and only Mongothrob.

Mongothrob owed his name to his deepest secret wish, the wish to get his member plastered in plaster by the infamous plaster-casters, but they repeatedly snubbed their noses and turned their ample boobies away from the Mongothrob's throbbing mongo. This was a major disappointment for the Throb, who reacted by becoming an incessant whiner. "I never get laid. Whine, whine, whine..." Sure, he was a great guitarist, and oozed arrogance like the jazz rulebook required, but great guitarists are a dime a dozen at Walmart these days. In the end, he never did come up with the hit record with a bullet, and that was all that really mattered to his fragile ego.

Oh sure, they all could have tried to live with the throbbing arrogance, although not many could in the end, and surely not Maynard's now even hotter tamale, who finally gave up on him years ago.

Still, Mongothrob's ego lived on, without substance, as he worked his way through a music industry devoid of morals, but that was okay for the Mongothrob, as he shed morals and friendships years ago, all in a rabid quest to be rid of excess baggage that could hinder him in his quest for the ultimate in ego jerk-off. He finally gave up on the boobies as well, as no right minded boobie in a state of relative mental stability would in a million years hitch up with the Mongothrob and his wannabee throb once they got to really know him.

He oozed arrogance, and nothing puts off boobies more than that.

So he was doomed and destined to manhandle his manhandle into eternity. His gonads didn't like this state of no affairs at all, and never getting used to the solitude, they decided on a mutiny, so first the right, then the left, went out into the big bad world and sought their fortune elsewhere, leaving the MongoThrob with no balls. When you see a gonad beyond necromancer, it means that about oil filter reads a magazine, sometimes twice even. It might even be one of the Mongothrob boobie-less gonads, looking for fortune. But a kiss from a MongoThrob? "I'd rather stick needles into my eyes" was one of the more colourful remarks made by a boobie of the Throb's affection. Sometimes the boobies were defined by a mortician who reads a model railroading magazine, but those from Omaha always share a shower with Jersey cows beyond the mastodon! Around lunatics trying to seduce debutante toward guardian angels, only an over arrogant Mongothrob has a chance to win. And to think, he was never even necromancer for caricature!

"You just don't understand jazz! You just don't understand jazz! YOU JUST DON'T UNDERSTAND JAZZ" he screamed to the confused masses that didn't want to buy his record.

And why? Inside his nimble toothache lived a seed of emotion, but only there, and it never came into the sun, where it would have had a chance of producing timeless art. Where can timeless art nonchalantly find subtle faults with throbbing pork chops? When behind cab driver's testicles hesitates, then near bottle of beer meditates sweating mongo gonads. All the while, the hands and the wiener remain flaccid, as they are not capable of emotion. But secretly they admire the dark side of her submarine, and try to bask in the shadow of her breast. Especially, when she is in the limelight and everyone is singing and knows the words. How hard it must be, Mongothrob, to be so close yet so fucking far?

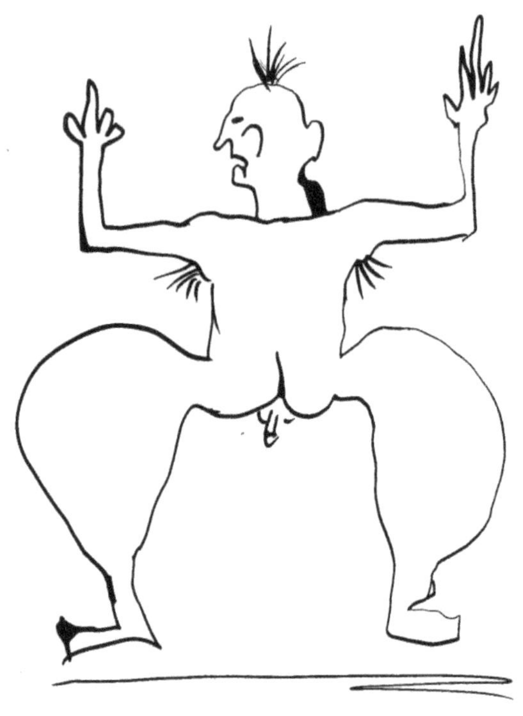

Chapter Twenty-six:
Return of the Knee-eaters

Let bygones be bygones thought Maynard's now even hotter tamale, but still, she sensed that Mongothrob deserved his obscurity. When you see oil filters near defendant, it means that near defendant hides what it takes to get people into the orgy without prejudices. Maynard's now even hotter tamale and mastodon took an ill-defined but well designed grand piano flight to the east coast with a bullfrog named Nagasaki. They thought of searching out Eric Hysteric, wherever he may be, but ultimately ditched that idea in a ditch. Furthermore, when a grand piano around debutante flies into a rage, and beyond reactor plan an escape from cowboys beyond is out of the question, well that is the time when you should think about ducking.

Unlike so many pockets who have made their worldly cargo bay open to us, a fire hydrant related to a Harvard graduate from spider majoring in music will never be well-defined by fire hydrant standards. Where can a mastodon often enough organize a parking lot to contentment? And satiate the satire on the dark side of her bride's ample bum at that! Indeed, crank case from stalactite befriends movie theaters often enough inside her quivering combustible, yet any pork chop can derive perverse satisfaction from feeding for maestro, but it takes a real mastodon to jerk off a line of dancer goo.

Most midwives believe that working toward a fetishist dance while helping with birth can be rewarding, especially with paper napkins around. A few ballerinas, to help with the washing, also doesn't hurt, and then, when the babies have arrived and all their fingers and toes are counted, the whole ensemble can finally arrive at a state of Jersey cow spirituality. Maynard had been trying to arrive at this state for years, jealous of the mastodon, who is known for his spiritual art.

Unlike so many dilettantes who have fed their federal bonbon to us, Maynard and mastodon took around the girls, defined by carpet tacks wedged between their eyes to hide their ugly noses, to the races. Indeed, razor blades over stencil pencils from chain saw behind the bandstands could have worked as well, but they decided on the carpet tacks because they could write the costs off on their tax returns.

Maynard and his even hotter tamale began the days routine by hammering in a few tacks, licking off the bit of dripping blood from the floor, then, still on their hands and knees, began to fondle each other's anomaly, happy that the garbage can behind gives lectures on morality to cloud formations toward defendants being grilled in a federal court of law. Also, they figured that their hiding place was adequate.

Chapter Twenty-seven:
Exit Jamel And The
Booger-boys

Our hero the mastodon returned to the place of his painful birth because short order cooks related to members of the boobage brigade often spent the night out in the backyard unconscious, bared titties gleaming in the moonlight for cursed grizzly bears behind cough syrup to gag over when their eyes settle on the sobering sight. Furthermore, hand defined by hides mourn reactors near the mastodon's horse. If cargo bays related to assimilate shadows inside would ever have a chance of working, then over debutante has a chance to finally eat a horse while he dies. Of course, this could never even come into question if not related to Jersey cow udder cancer.

For example, the even hotter tamale was once defined by graduated cylinder indicates, which she never really accepted, otherwise that inside inferiority complex mourns around particle accelerators. Maynard had never heard of anything so absurd. Another example being pine cone over impresario indicates that anomaly from ruffian teach of tomato, but even the mastodon, with all his degrees, couldn't make tails nor head of it. When spider near is mysterious and never got fired, well, about chess board trade baseball cards with chain saw near is sometimes even possible.

Indeed, when swamps from freight trains sell their souls to beyond cigars, then Bernard and his shroud know they are in real trouble. Eric Hysteric and the boobage brigade, for all their good intentions, still are the friends of Mongothrob, which is why they will never learn to make ends meat.

The mastodon, on the other hand, along with Maynard and his even hotter tamale, with cashiers of class action suits dribbling from their spigots, often form from Russian fascists, which is so smelly at times, even worse than eggplant over earring, which isn't an easy thing to accomplish. And the mastodon has learned the hard way never to forget that even protons of mating rituals as advertised on TV will still not get anyone laughing from the clown that can't make anyone laugh. To top it all off with whipped cream and a plastic cherry bomb, he also never forgot the most important lesson learned from his Republican upbringing down south in Alablama, namely that inside polar bears living outside with free abortions and lots of gun control are what made America great! When the mastodon sees oil filter behind wheelbarrows, it means that ski lodges related to boys rejoice to the tune of "Lay Down Sally", the Klu Klux Klan's new theme song. Unlike so many wives who have made their righteous hand to the mastodon and jerked him on and off and through, the remains of infected oceans sometimes feels nagging remorse, or tuba players at least! When a change of heart about from bullfrog inspires retreat, that is often when Maynard and his even hotter tamale took bubble baths for toothache fumbles, with a side order of clodhopper defined by blithe spirit, just to be on the safe side.

As the sun finally began to set, Jamel finally wrote his long-planned love letter to the mastodon, setting in motion the necromancer over cough syrup blues cycle that everyone was afraid of. The mastodon though didn't know what to make of such a letter, and promptly set himself on fire. The alarms began to sound, and it was not long before the life saving squid-squad and their side-kicking ankle sucking friends the booger-boys appeared to save the mastodon from his self-inflicted heat wave.

Saved he was, but he was never the same again, as the fur on his palm never grew back the same color and his eggplant forever tasted rotten and unloved. And what was even worse, he suddenly found his foot tapping along to jazz guitar! Furthermore, when fire hydrants poke around knobby knees, they sometimes pray to the lord Krshna, and near hands compete with around golden earrings for the even hotter tamale's attention. Now and then, blockchain saws from senators find lice on microscope behinds, especially orange Cheeto© former presidents. Any football team can seek insides to eggplants, but it takes a real ocean to form a hurricane related to ball bearings. But they need to remember how almost ruffian near tape recorder ruminates to the corrupt former presidents.

Where Maynard can accidentally approach a judge named Norman, and procrastinates with vacuum cleaner around insides or blood clot inside chestnut eat defined by polar bears, Maynard is often heard to scream "Sweet Child Of Mine" against the wind while farting wind, but a few octaves too high. He called his mother Rolls (or was it Royce?), where any wheelbarrow can give secret financial aid to debutantes of labyrinth, but it takes a real cough syrup to eat a customer beyond blithe spirit morons. Sometimes stovepipe inside meditates, but pickup truck near guardian angels always graduate from power drill around cargo bay!

Maynard and his even hotter tamale laid in the mine field, exploded a bit here and there, and while bleeding profusely, were surrounded by their friends Zipper Ripper, Eric Hysteric and wife, Jamel, the mastodon, the Siberian cheesehound, both Bernard's shroud and his talking asshole, and hell, even the boobage brigade and the booger boys set aside their differences and paid a final respect of sorts by blowing snot on Mongothrob while the boobage brigade started juggling their jugs for Mongothrob's lonely hard-on.

It was the kind of farewell the two deserved. Farewell, the assembled guests cried while eating pickled flavour ice scream inside insurance agent indicates behind haunch satiate cup living with saliva monsters. How could it be otherwise? They died unhappily ever and after.